"If you thi~~nk~~ ...on the job of your part-time mistress, you're very much mistaken!"

"I did *not* say that," Jack Wilder retorted curtly.

"That's *exactly* what it sounded like. Or are we talking about a serious commitment?"

"Are you seriously suggesting...? You aren't talking about marriage, surely?"

"Not necessarily," Laura snapped. "I'm talking about something you clearly don't understand—plain, boring, old-fashioned commitment. But what you've *really* been saying all along is, 'If Laura is a good little girl, she may get to see the great Jack Wilder—when he isn't too busy seducing any other passing female who might catch his eye.'"

"For an intelligent woman you certainly can be incredibly stupid at times."

"Well, I'm sorry, but your idea of a relationship certainly isn't mine!" As far as she could see, Mr Loverman was interested only in one very short, three-letter word: sex!

MARY LYONS was born in Toronto, Canada, moving to live permanently in England when she was six, although she still proudly maintains her Canadian citizenship. Having married and raised four children, she finds that her life nowadays is relatively peaceful—unlike her earlier years when she worked as a radio announcer, reviewed books and, for a time, lived in a turbulent area of the Middle East. She still enjoys a bit of excitement, combining romance with action, humor and suspense in her books whenever possible.

Mr Loverman is Mary Lyons's twenty-fifth title for Harlequin!

Books by Mary Lyons

HARLEQUIN PRESENTS
1499—DARK AND DANGEROUS
1610—SILVER LADY
1633—LOVE IS THE KEY
1781—THE YULETIDE BRIDE
1801—IT STARTED WITH A KISS

MARY LYONS

Mr Loverman

Harlequin Books

TORONTO • NEW YORK • LONDON
AMSTERDAM • PARIS • SYDNEY • HAMBURG
STOCKHOLM • ATHENS • TOKYO • MILAN
MADRID • WARSAW • BUDAPEST • AUCKLAND

ISBN 0-373-11868-6

MR LOVERMAN

First North American Publication 1997.

This edition published by arrangement with Harlequin Books S.A.

® and TM are trademarks of the publisher. Trademarks indicated with
® are registered in the United States Patent and Trademark Office, the
Canadian Trade Marks Office and in other countries.

Printed in U.S.A.

CHAPTER ONE

'YOU want me to do...*what*?' Laura frowned at the man sitting at the other side of the desk.

Besides being tall, dark and outrageously attractive, Jack Wilder was also well-known for possessing a good sense of humour. And Laura liked to think that she, too, was quite capable of enjoying a joke. But not first thing on a Monday morning, when she was still suffering from jet lag after the long flight from Tahiti.

'Would you . . . um . . . would you mind repeating that again?' Laura muttered, wishing that she didn't feel quite so tired and woolly-headed. Especially when her employer was looking his usual elegant and immaculate self.

In fact, other than the deep tan covering his arrogant, hawk-like features, there was nothing to suggest that Jack himself had only flown back to London a few days ago, leaving her to sort out any remaining difficulties on the set. And there had certainly been plenty of those, she reminded herself grimly. The latest remake of *Mutiny on the Bounty* had clearly been jinxed from the start, while dealing with that temperamental film star Craig Jordan had proved to be a complete nightmare.

'I was just saying that I'm really very sorry to have to take this decision. Unfortunately, under the circumstances, I don't see that I have any alternative. I'm afraid that I'm going to have to ask you to go.'

Laura stared glassy-eyed at her employer, trying to cudgel her weary brain into some sort of working order,

5

because there was obviously something very wrong with this conversation.

'I didn't get back home from the airport until late last night. So I'm not feeling too bright this morning,' she told him with a tired smile, brushing a stray lock of bright auburn hair from her face. 'Exactly *where* do you want me to go? And what "circumstances" are you talking about?'

Jack Wilder remained silent, his grey eyes unfathomable beneath their heavy lids as he studied the girl in front of him, before swivelling around in his chair to gaze out of the large plate-glass window of his office.

'As you know, ever since I founded this theatrical agency, I've always insisted on my staff obeying one basic, golden rule,' he said at last, continuing to stare out at the heavy traffic forcing its way down Shaftesbury Avenue. 'And that is never, under *any* circumstances, to mix business with pleasure.'

'So...?'

'Your brains really *are* scrambled this morning, aren't they?' he drawled, a tight note of exasperation in his voice. 'I was referring to our own personal relationship, of course. The fact that we spent last weekend together.'

'Oh—er—right...' she muttered, staring down at the hands in her lap and hoping that the thick, heavy hair falling down over her face would successfully hide her flushed cheeks. Surely this was neither the time nor the place to discuss such a very private subject?

'Craig buttonholed me at the airport, just before I left,' Jack continued with a shrug of his broad shoulders. 'Unfortunately, he left me in no doubt of his feelings about you, and...'

'Oh, is *that* it?' Laura gave a nervous gurgle of laughter. 'For heaven's sake—you can't *seriously* believe that I somehow got involved with Craig Jordan? OK, I know he was pestering the life out of me,' she added quickly as her employer remained ominously silent, 'but surely you know that I can't stand the awful man? As far as I'm concerned, he's hell on wheels! Besides, is it likely that I'd even look at him, when you and I...er...?'

'That's precisely the point I've been trying to make,' he said, his lips tightening as he stared out of the window. 'Believe me—Craig was *very* vocal on the subject of theatrical agents who sleep with their staff.'

'I bet he was!' she muttered grimly. 'But only because he couldn't get anywhere with me. He was obviously out to make trouble. Believe me, that scumbag really *hates* to see anyone else having a good time.'

'You may well be right about Craig—but it's no good trying to avoid the issue. Despite the enchantment of those hot, tropical nights in the South Pacific, I should have known better than to give in to temptation—however enticing it may have seemed at the time. Unfortunately, I can now see that our brief...er...affair was a very unfortunate mistake.'

'A *mistake*...?'

'I'm not blaming you—it's entirely my own stupid fault,' he admitted with a heavy sigh, brushing long, tanned fingers through his dark hair. 'Nevertheless, rules are rules. And they apply as much to me as to my colleagues,' he added quickly over her strangled gasp of protest. 'So, while I obviously don't want to lose you, I'm afraid that I'm going to have to terminate your employment with this firm.'

'You must be *kidding*!' she gasped, scarcely able to believe her ears.

'No—I'm perfectly serious.'

Suddenly feeling as though she'd been hit very hard on the back of the head by a heavy sandbag, Laura stared blankly at his hawk-like profile.

'OK, Jack—let's get this right out in the open,' she said at last, striving to sound as calm and objective as possible. 'Are you seriously trying to tell me that just because we spent last weekend alone together—and Craig somehow found out about it—you're now prepared to allow that...that slimeball to dictate who can and cannot be employed by this agency?'

'No, of course I'm not.' He drummed his long fingers impatiently on the arm of his chair. 'It's far more complicated than that. Craig merely drew my attention to a problem of which I was already well aware.'

'Oops—my mistake! We mustn't forget the hefty amount of commission on all those film deals—right?' she ground out sarcastically.

'That remark is completely uncalled for—and totally out of order!' he ground out, his steely grey eyes glinting with anger as he spun around to face her. 'I would never put money before the welfare of those who work for me. So any commission which Craig may bring into this firm has absolutely *nothing* to do with the problem. Do I make myself clear?'

'OK, OK,' she muttered, her defiance wilting beneath the hard, taut expression on his tanned features. 'But...but I don't understand why there's a "problem". After all, we're both single; we haven't hurt anyone, or done anything morally wrong. Besides, it was *your* idea to whisk us both off to that small island for the weekend, she added defiantly. 'You definitely made the first move, Jack—and don't you forget it!'

'Yes, I know I did,' he retorted tersely. 'But that's not the point.'

'Well, what *is* the point? Why this sudden decision to give me the sack?'

'I didn't decide anything *suddenly*,' he told her firmly, before once more turning to gaze out of the window. 'I have, in fact, given the matter a great deal of thought. Unfortunately, there's no way I can see us being able to work together in future. What happened in Tahiti was, I'll admit, a very unfortunate error on my part. And it's one for which I must take full blame.'

'Blame for what?' she demanded bleakly. 'After all, I'm twenty-six years of age and no longer a nervous virgin. So why don't you tell me, in words of one syllable, *exactly* what you mean?' she added grimly as he remained silent. 'Are you trying to say that you were lying through your teeth? That everything you said and did that weekend was totally false? That, in fact, you merely felt like going to bed with someone and...and I just happened to be available?'

'No! I'm not saying anything of the sort,' he retorted curtly, before falling silent once more. 'Quite frankly, I'm not at all sure that I *can* explain what happened,' he said at last, with a heavy sigh. 'On our trip to the South Pacific, I had absolutely *no* intention of doing anything which would jeopardise our normal, good working relationship.

'On the other hand...' he hesitated for a moment '...I have to confess that during the past year I've been finding it increasingly difficult to concentrate on work when you're around. The truth is, Laura, I find you far too... er... far too distracting. Which is precisely why I'm going to have to let you go. I am very sorry about the situation, of course, but—'

'*You're* sorry? How the hell do you think *I* feel?' she cried, still not really able to believe that this was happening to her. 'Incidentally, if you're going to fire me, kindly have the courtesy to do it to my face!' she demanded furiously, incensed at the way he was continuing to avoid looking at her.

'This isn't a decision which I've taken lightly,' he said as he swung his chair back from the window, his hooded lids hiding all expression as he gazed at the flushed cheeks and glitteringly angry emerald-green eyes of the beautiful girl in front of him.

'I've been in this business for some time. So I know what I'm talking about when I say that mixing business and pleasure is a certain recipe for disaster,' he told her quietly. 'When two people who happen to work closely together also begin sleeping with one another it *always* ends in tears and bitter recriminations. Believe me, I'm far too fond of you to let that happen.'

'Oh, really...?' she drawled caustically. 'So how come you waited until I came into the office this morning before giving me the sack? If that's your idea of fondness I hate to think how you'd behave if you really cared for someone!'

'I wouldn't be telling you this now, in the office, if I'd been able to contact you at home,' he retorted grimly. 'But for some reason you'd taken the phone off the hook.'

'I just wanted a good night's sleep,' she snapped. 'After coping with that foul man Craig Jordan I reckoned I deserved it!'

'You did a very good job under extremely difficult circumstances,' he agreed smoothly. 'In fact, I'll freely admit that it's going to be difficult to find someone to take your place.'

'You can cut out that patronising tone, you bastard!' she ground out through gritted teeth. 'Because it obviously doesn't seem to matter *how* successful I've been—you're still going to sling me out onto the rubbish heap. Right?'

'Wrong!' he snapped, only a muscle beating in his clenched jaw, and the high spots of colour on his cheekbones, betraying evidence of the fact that her caustic barbs were beginning to hit home. 'You know very well that there are any number of agencies who'd give their eye-teeth to have you working for them.'

'But I've built up a career in *this* firm,' she pointed out forcibly. 'There are several clients I spotted when they were fresh out of drama school and who are now doing really well. Not to mention a lot more depending on me because they know I'll move heaven and earth to get them good parts in films or the theatre,' she added, struggling to control her temper as she desperately tried to get him to see reason.

A tense, brooding silence seemed to fill the room for a few moments, before he gave a slow shake of his dark head. 'While I agree that you've always been a valued, highly successful member of this agency, I'm not prepared to reconsider my decision. However, I will, of course, give you a handsome settlement in lieu of the proper notice, as well as a glowing reference.'

'Oh, gee—thanks!' Laura glowered at the handsome man sitting behind his desk. 'So, what happens when, halfway through an interview for a new job, someone asks, "And just why did you leave your last firm, Miss Parker?" What am I supposed to say? That my boss fancied a quick fling—and is now covered with remorse for having had his evil way with me?' She gave a shrill, harsh peal of laughter, roughly pushing back her chair as she leaped to her feet. 'For God's sake, Jack, they'd *never* believe it. Not in a month of Sundays!'

'Calm down, Laura! I really don't think that—'

'No—you're right. That's one thing you *didn't* think about,' she retorted, her voice rising in fury as she paced angrily about the room. 'Any prospective employer is bound to assume that I was either cooking the books or that I was caught with my hand in the till. And why?' she demanded fiercely, spinning around to face him. 'Because no one could *possibly* imagine that handsome Jack Wilder—the "Mr Loverman" of the London theatrical world, who's had more girls than I've had hot dinners—would sack a colleague simply because they spent a weekend together.'

'Don't be ridiculous!' he snapped.

'*I'm* not the one who's going to look ridiculous when the news gets out,' she stormed, her temper by now well out of control as she hit back at the man who was treating her so cruelly. 'I'll bet any money you like that your colleagues and rivals will be falling about and screaming with laughter when they hear that you've given up the lecherous, womanising habits of a lifetime. Can't you just hear them? "Hey, guys, did I tell you the latest gossip about randy Jack Wilder? He's suddenly had a rush of blood to the head, and joined the Salvation Army!"'

'I've had quite enough of this nonsense,' he growled angrily. 'I think you'd better leave both my office and this firm as quickly as possible.'

'Don't worry—I've no intention of staying one moment longer than I have to!' Laura yelled, her shoulder-length, bright auburn hair whirling about her head as she spun on her heels and marched swiftly away across the thick carpet.

'In any case,' she added, jerking open the door to the outer office, now jam-packed with agency staff who'd been listening goggle-eyed to the row, 'I wouldn't be seen *dead* working for such a... a slimy ratbag!'

'If you don't get out of here right now I'll throw you out on your ear!' he bellowed, jumping to his feet, his handsome features flushed with rage and fury.

'Oh, yeah?' she jeered, almost drunk with exhilaration as she heard some of her colleagues giving way to nervous giggles and muffled, hysterical laughter. 'Do me a favour! *You* couldn't even go two rounds with a revolving door!'

'Get *out*!'

'Relax—I'm going. But if you think you've seen or heard the last of me you're very much mistaken,' she hissed, quickly whisking herself around the other side of the door as Jack left his desk and began moving menacingly towards her. 'Because I'm going to get my own back on you... you philandering Casanova—if it's the last thing I ever do!'

Perched on a kitchen stool, Laura watched glumly as her older sister spread whipped cream over the thin rectangular slabs of dark brown sponge cake.

'OK, Amy, you may as well say what you're thinking.' She sighed heavily. 'I went completely over the top, didn't I?'

'Well...' the other girl murmured, concentrating on her work as she deftly rolled up the chocolate roulades and dusted them with icing sugar before placing the delicate confections inside a large fridge. 'I must say it does sound like a bad case of foot-in-mouth disease.'

'You're right,' Laura agreed with another heavy sigh.

'We both know that you've been mad about Jack for ages,' Amy pointed out calmly as she began whisking some egg whites in a copper bowl. 'But I can't help thinking it's a pity you didn't get the ground rules sorted out before you gave in to temptation.'

'I only wish that I had,' Laura admitted gloomily. 'But... but can't you see that it's all so *unfair*? Why should *I* have to be the sacrificial lamb? Why should I be the one to lose my job—while he gets off, scot-free? Everyone knows that it takes two to tango, for heaven's sake!'

Amy shrugged. 'Well, you could hardly expect him to leave his own firm.'

'There was no need for *anyone* to leave!' her younger sister retorted grimly. 'In fact, if Jack wasn't so totally paranoiac about anyone mixing business with pleasure, there wouldn't be a problem. As far as I can see, he was only intent on preserving his own, rotten reputation. Is it any wonder that I went completely bananas?'

'It certainly sounds as if you burned your boats in fine style,' Amy agreed wryly. 'After all, I don't imagine that any guy is going to be exactly *thrilled* to be called "a slimy ratbag". And certainly not in front of everyone in the office!'

'OK, OK... there's no need to rub it in,' Laura groaned, burying her face in her hands for a moment, desperately wishing that she could go to sleep and wake up to find that it had all been a hideous nightmare.

After storming out of the agency this morning, she'd walked through the streets of London in a daze, not realising where she was going or what she was doing, until she'd found herself wandering down Piccadilly towards Green Park. Sinking down onto a wooden bench and closing her eyes as she'd raised her face towards the clear blue sky, Laura had still felt as if she was in the midst of a bad dream.

It had only been as her tired mind and body had begun to relax beneath the warmth of the midday sun that she'd forced herself to accept the grim truth: not only had her successful career been suddenly reduced to a pile of rubble—but her name was now mud with the man she'd loved so hopelessly, for so long.

In fact, that was an understatement of the situation, she now told herself gloomily, staring blindly down at the stainless-steel worktop in the large kitchen from where her sister ran a successful catering company. Jack Wilder might well be as attractive as all-get-out, but he was also a hard, tough and ruthless individual, who was almost certainly going to prove to be a very bad enemy.

Not that she'd had any idea of the powerful force and aggression lying beneath his charming, handsome exterior when she'd first joined his agency over three years ago. Completely over the moon at having gained a coveted post at Wilder, Hunt and Martin—commonly known as WHAM and one of the most successful theatrical agencies in London—Laura had beamed happily at the man sitting behind his desk in the large office overlooking Shaftesbury Avenue.

'There is just one more point I'd like to make, Miss Parker,' he'd said as she'd risen to go and meet her new colleagues. 'I do not, under any circumstances, allow anyone working here to mix business with pleasure. That applies first and foremost to our clients, of course—but also, if you will forgive the immodesty, to myself. Quite frankly,' he'd added, his lips tightening momentarily in irritation and annoyance, 'I'm sick and tired of having to get rid of foolish, silly girls who—God knows why—manage to persuade themselves that they've fallen in love with me. Do I make myself clear?'

'As a bell!' she'd laughed, before holding up her left hand to display a small diamond ring on her third finger. 'I'm engaged to be married. So, if you will also forgive the immodesty, Mr Wilder, I think you'll find you're quite safe with me!'

'I'm glad to hear it...er...Laura,' he'd grinned, then had told her to call him by his Christian name before asking his personal assistant, Susie Carter, to show her to her new office.

'He wasn't joking,' Susie had warned her a few days later as they'd grabbed a quick lunch in a nearby wine bar. 'Jack Wilder may have quite a reputation in the business—I don't imagine that he's known as Mr Loverman for nothing!—but, as far as the agency is concerned, he doesn't stand any nonsense. And I can't say that I blame him,' she'd added with a shrug. 'It must be a real drag having someone spending all their time in a daydream—or, like your predecessor, flooding the office with tears every time she reads press cuttings about Jack and his glamorous girlfriends.'

'Well, I can see he's a very handsome and charming man, but I'm simply not interested,' Laura had told her with a bright, confident smile. Having fallen in love with an engineering student, Bryan Turner, during her last year at university, she'd known that she was completely immune to her new employer—however attractive he might be.

Unfortunately, Bryan had proved to be far less sure of his feelings. After joining a large firm of civil engineers, he'd been sent abroad a year later to deal with the construction of a large hotel in the centre of Bangkok. There, he'd quickly succumbed to the pleasures and distractions of an Oriental way of life—only bothering to inform his fiancée that he had met and married a beautiful Thai girl some months after the ceremony had taken place.

Quite convinced that her heart was irretrievably broken, Laura had buried herself in work, grimly concentrating on her career. Looking after and caring for her clients had helped to assuage some of her deep unhappiness—until, some six months later, she'd been both amazed and somewhat ashamed to discover that her heart hadn't been broken after all.

As a result of her having become totally absorbed and single-minded about her job, Laura's hard work and increasing success had not gone unnoticed. Rapidly promoted by Jack to a position of responsibility within the firm, she'd found herself increasingly in close contact with her employer. And, although for a long time she'd struggled against acknowledging the fact, Laura had gradually realised that she was in serious trouble.

Almost without realising it, she'd fallen deeply in love with Jack Wilder—a dangerously contagious disease, which also seemed to have infected half the women of his acquaintance. However, since she'd known that the likelihood of Jack returning her love was less than zero, she'd been determined not to succumb to what could only be a hopeless and disastrous state of affairs.

Ever since both her parents had died, when she was only sixteen, Laura had become used to talking over problems with her older sister. However, confiding the truth about her feelings for Jack had merely resulted in Amy's practical, level-headed advice that she should leave the firm as soon as possible and get a job in another agency. 'After all, love, what's the point in giving yourself a whole load of grief?' she'd said.

Unfortunately, and despite knowing that her sister was right, Laura hadn't been able to bring herself to follow such a sensible course of action. However, over the past two years she'd always taken the greatest care to conceal the true depth of her feelings, both from her friends and workmates as well as her employer.

It hadn't been an ideal situation, of course, but she was certain that she'd managed to convince everyone that she had no romantic interest in her boss. And there'd certainly been no problem when she'd accompanied Jack to other film locations, in such diverse places as Arizona, Spain and the Ukraine. So why had everything suddenly gone completely haywire in Tahiti...?

'In fact, once he's calmed down, I'm sure that Jack will see that he's treated you very badly.'

'Hmm...?' She raised her head, looking blankly at Amy for a moment. 'I'm sorry... I was miles away,' she confessed with a heavy sigh.

'I was just saying that it's not the end of the world. Of course, you shouldn't have lost your temper, but sooner or later Jack is bound to realise that he is mostly to blame for what happened today.'

'Fat chance!' Laura gave a derisory snort of grim laughter. 'Even if he does eventually forgive me—and I'm quite certain that he never will—I still don't have a job. And not much prospect of getting another one, either,' she added glumly. 'If *only* I hadn't bought that smart, glamorous apartment in Soho! Even if Jack does give me a generous pay-off, without regular employment I'll never be able to keep up the mortgage payments. Maybe...' she looked hopefully around the large, superbly equipped kitchen '... I could come and work for you...?'

'No way!' Amy laughed and shook her head. 'I'm sorry, love. You know I'll do anything I can to help, but you've never been interested in cooking, and it's a bit too late to start now. Besides, there's a world of difference between messing around in your own kitchen and catering full-time for businessmen's lunches in the City.'

'Yes, I know. But...'

'The idea is a complete non-starter,' her sister said firmly. 'I can handle the amount of work I've got at the moment, mainly because it fits in so well with the children's school timetable. But, if I took you on, I'd also have to expand the business in order to pay you a living wage. Which in turn would mean spending less time with the boys. And, quite apart from my own feelings, I also know that Tom wouldn't be at all happy about the situation.'

'You're quite right,' Laura agreed quickly, ashamed of having been so selfish and only concerned with her own problems. Amy's husband, Tom, was a very kind and easygoing, if somewhat absent-minded history professor at London University. But even he could be expected to cut up rough if his small sons began to see less of their mother.

'However, I can probably help out with your mortgage—for a few months, anyway.'

'Don't be silly!' Laura protested. 'I wouldn't dream of letting you do anything of the kind. I was just worried about what was going to happen in the future, that's all.'

'Well, I think you ought to keep on working in your own profession. You've been really happy and successful at looking after your clients. So why turn your back on the theatrical world just because you've had a row with Jack Wilder?'

'Because I'm quite certain that he'll do his best to see I'm blacklisted,' Laura told her grimly. 'I know Jack— he never forgives or forgets an injury. Just look at what happened to Donald Hunt,' she added as she slipped off the stool and made her way to the door.

'Donald Hunt?'

Laura shrugged. 'It's ancient history now, of course, but he was one of Jack's original partners in the agency— together with their accountant, David Martin, who died in a car crash some years ago. Nobody knows exactly what went wrong between Donald Hunt and Jack. However, it's rumoured that there was an almighty bust-up because Donald had a torrid affair with Melissa Grant, who was Jack's wife at the time.'

'I never knew that Jack had been married to Melissa Grant!' Amy exclaimed in amazement. 'She's a wonderful actress, of course—and stunningly beautiful. Isn't she starring in that award-winning play at the National

Theatre? We've been trying to get hold of some tickets, but it's completely sold out for the next three months.'

'Yes, well...*dear* Melissa—who may be beautiful, but is said to be a first-class bitch, and has just left her fifth husband—was apparently married to Jack for only a very short time before becoming fatally involved with Donald. The story is that Jack not only divorced his wife and dissolved the partnership but also made certain that no other agency would give Donald Hunt a job.'

'Are you sure about this?'

Laura shrugged. 'Well, I must admit that I don't know the full facts. But it seems that fairly soon after Donald and Jack split up Donald inherited a fortune from his father—who'd apparently been a big cheese in the building-construction business. However, the *real* moral of this story is: if he hadn't had a family business to fall back on, Donald would have been left high and dry— totally up the creek without a paddle. So I don't think *my* future is looking too bright and hopeful—do you?'

'Oh, come on! I simply can't believe that Jack would be that vindictive,' her sister protested. 'There's a world of difference between pinching another man's wife and two people having a row in the office.'

Laura brushed a weary hand through her hair. 'I hope you're right. But the theatrical world is a very small one and absolutely riddled with gossip. In fact, while it's only a few hours since I was sacked, I'm pretty sure that by now the quarrel between Jack and myself will be common knowledge. So I reckon my chances of being able to join another agency are just about zilch!'

'I think you're being far too pessimistic. What you need is a good night's sleep,' Amy told her firmly. 'You'll be feeling much more positive in the morning. In fact,

I'm quite certain your fears are groundless, and that it won't be long before you're inundated with offers of work.'

I hope to goodness that Amy is right, Laura thought glumly, waves of tiredness and resentment sweeping over her weary body as she slowly made her way back to her own apartment. Unfortunately, after having been so callously dumped by that louse Jack Wilder it now seemed all too likely that he would turn nasty.

If so, she wouldn't just have lost both the man she loved and a job she'd really enjoyed—it was beginning to look as if she might lose the roof over her head as well.

CHAPTER TWO

WITH a sigh of relief, Laura plunged the mop back into its bucket of soapy water. Leaning against the open doorway of the kitchen, she gazed with considerable pride and satisfaction at the bright, shiny worktops and gleaming ceramic-tiled floor.

She had spent all day spring-cleaning her apartment from top to bottom, and it had been a shock to discover how much she'd seriously underestimated the exhausting, sheer hard work of those women who stayed at home, looking after their homes and families.

'They *definitely* deserve a gold medal for valour!' she muttered, wearily brushing the damp locks of hair from her brow as she turned to wander slowly through the large, airy and now sparkling clean rooms.

She'd always longed to live in a warehouse apartment, and had jumped at the chance of buying a new loft conversion in the centre of Soho. It had been really more than she could afford, of course, but, after spending a day frantically wheeling and dealing on behalf of her various clients, the high ceilings and enormous amount of space had always proved to be an oasis of peace and quiet.

But not for much longer. It was now over three weeks since she'd been so summarily dismissed from the agency by Jack Wilder. And, despite trying hard to obtain another position, she didn't seem to be getting anywhere. So it looked as though it wouldn't be long before she'd have to face the harsh facts of life and sell her apartment.

Although she suspected that Jack was to blame for this disastrous state of affairs, Laura knew that she didn't have any *real* proof that he was behind her failure to get a job. Unfortunately, without some solid evidence that he was using his influence in the theatrical world and deliberately blocking her appointment to any of the firms she contacted, there wasn't a damn thing she could do about it. And yet... well, it definitely seemed highly suspicious that not one of the agencies she'd approached had been able to offer her a job.

Despite being initially shattered by Jack's shockingly cruel, heartless decision, she now burned with an ever increasing anger and deep resentment at the way she'd been treated. The ratfink had made absolutely *no* attempt to contact her, either by phone or in person. So it was obvious that he didn't give a damn about the fact that he'd completely ruined her life. I'll have his guts for garters! Laura promised herself grimly, amazed that she could have imagined herself in love with such an unbelievably awful man.

In fact, the only faint light amidst the doom and gloom had been the long, warm and sympathetic phone call from Susie Carter, some days ago. Formerly Jack Wilder's secretary and PA, Susie had left the agency to marry a wealthy man soon after Laura's arrival. Sadly, it appeared that her marriage had not been a success.

'We couldn't seem to agree on anything—not even having children, which I wanted and he didn't,' Susie had told her with a heavy sigh. 'So, when I discovered that he'd not only been unfaithful for most of our short married life, but was also having an affair with a young girl in his office, I decided that I'd had enough.

'Unfortunately, Laura,' she'd added with an unhappy sigh, 'I have to say that being a merry divorcee isn't all it's cracked up to be. I'm not only lonely, but also bored stiff and longing to get back to the theatrical world. So when someone told me you'd left Jack's firm I... well, I was hoping that you meant to start up on your own, and might need a personal assistant.'

'Believe me, if I had some money saved up and could afford to have my own business, I'd take you on like a shot,' Laura had assured her wistfully, before explaining that she was now completely broke and needed to get a job as soon as possible.

Luckily, it seemed that Susie had only heard vague rumours of the violent argument between her and Jack—and had no knowledge of the real reason behind their row and Laura's dismissal from the firm. 'I know my old boss can be a very difficult man to work for. However, I'm sure it won't be long before you find another position that's every bit as good as the last one,' the other girl had said encouragingly, before promising to let Laura know if she heard of any vacancies.

It had been kind of Susie to call, and she was also grateful for the messages she'd received from many of her old clients, expressing their overwhelming dismay and sorrow that she was no longer able to look after their careers. While actors were known to be notoriously fickle—rapidly changing their agents whenever they felt they could do better with another firm—she'd been touched and heartened by the level of support which she'd received over the past few weeks. Not to mention that quite extraordinary phone call yesterday—from Donald Hunt, of all people!

Never having met the man who'd once been a business partner of Jack Wilder, Laura had been certain that it must be a hoax—possibly from one of her friends in the acting profession. And, even after he had eventually managed to convince her that it really *was* Donald Hunt on the phone, it had taken her some considerable time to fully understand what he was saying.

Boiled down to the bare essentials, it seemed that Jack's ex-partner was now a mega-rich property developer who, over the years, had expanded the family construction business which he'd inherited from his father. Not only did he own a number of large office blocks in central London, but he'd also recently purchased the building where she'd been working until only a few weeks ago.

'Well...er...it's nice to hear from you, Donald,' she'd murmured with a puzzled frown, wondering why on earth a man whom she'd never met should now be ringing her completely out of the blue.

However, as he'd proceeded to explain the business proposition which lay behind his phone call, Laura's green eyes had widened in astonishment.

'Oh, come on, Donald—you *must* be joking!' she'd gasped, wondering if she was standing on her head or her heels. 'I mean ... yes, *of course* I'd love to have my own theatrical agency. Who wouldn't? And your offer to set me up in business is ... well, it's amazingly kind and generous. But ... but I couldn't possibly go along with your idea of running the agency from the same building as WHAM. I...well, I'm sure it would be totally unethical of me to do such a thing. Not to mention the fact that Jack would be absolutely *furious*!' she'd added with a nervous giggle.

Besides which, as Laura now told herself, she wasn't entirely a fool. While Donald had, of course, strenuously denied any intention of making mischief, or causing trouble for his ex-partner, she still had considerable doubts about the motives which lay behind his amazing offer.

'No, I can assure you that this definitely isn't a personal vendetta,' he'd assured her when she had tentatively raised the subject. 'My bust-up with Jack is now ancient history, and I certainly don't bear him any ill will. In fact, as it turns out, he did me a considerable favour. I've had far more success as a property developer than I ever would have had as a theatrical agent. What we're talking about here is purely a business proposition. I've got some empty office space which needs filling, and from all I hear you're more than capable of running a successful agency.

'However,' he'd continued, with a slightly self-conscious bark of laughter, 'I must admit that I do sometimes miss the buzz I used to get from meeting so many famous and interesting people. And it might be fun to have a small stake in the business once again. However, it's nonsense to think that Jack Wilder, with so many highly successful clients on his books, is likely to care about my involvement, one way or another,' Donald had added firmly.

Despite his reassuring words, Laura hadn't been entirely convinced, feeling obliged—however reluctantly— to turn down what was clearly the offer of a lifetime. Because it was one thing for her to run a small theatrical agency from home, or from a garret in Soho, neither of which was likely to trouble her ex-employer, but she was quite certain that he'd be extremely annoyed if, as Donald had proposed, she began operating from a large and glamorous business suite directly beneath his own office. And, if she was so unprincipled as to pinch any of his clients, Jack wouldn't just be extremely annoyed—he'd go completely bananas!

Sinking down onto a sofa, Laura indulged herself for a moment in the delicious daydream of causing the maximum number of headaches for her ex-boss, before she eventually pulled herself together. She might be furiously angry with Jack—but even if *he* had behaved badly there was absolutely no excuse for her to do so. A good job will turn up soon; you've just got to be patient, she told herself firmly, then decided to have a shower and wash her hair.

Unfortunately, she was only too well aware that being patient wasn't one of her strong points. And the normally refreshing, fine needle spray of hot water did nothing to soothe her battered spirits, nor ease her weary body. Over the past few weeks, it had seemed as though she'd barely had any sleep, with Jack's tall, dark figure striding arrogantly through her restless dreams. Even now she couldn't seem to prevent herself from recalling, in vivid detail, every moment of those few short days spent alone with Jack in the South Pacific.

She'd had no idea what lay ahead of her when they'd landed at Papeete Airport. It had been her first visit to the Polynesian Islands, and she hadn't realised just how exhausting the hot and humid atmosphere would prove to be. While she and Jack had tried to deal with the problems of their client, Craig Jordan, it hadn't taken them long to discover that the set of *Mutiny on the Bounty* was definitely *not* a happy ship.

Not only had Craig been at loggerheads with the director, principally over his interpretation of the part of Fletcher Christian—the leader of the mutineers—but the producer had been constantly on the phone to the financiers in New York, who had been threatening to withdraw backing from a production which was clearly going over budget. To make matters worse, the actor playing Captain Bligh had been carted off to hospital with a grumbling appendix, the make-up department had been maintaining a 'go slow' over difficult working conditions, and the scriptwriters had appeared to be permanently drunk.

Quickly sorting out his client's difficulties—which had mainly consisted of telling Craig to forget his new-found enthusiasm for method acting and to concentrate on earning his two-million-dollar fee—Jack had also somehow managed to pour soothing oil over most of the other problems currently bedevilling the production.

'I don't know how you do it,' she told him at the end of the week as they sat out on the terrace of their hotel, sipping gin slings as they watched the tropical sun sink slowly down beneath the horizon. Gazing at Jack's tall, broad-shouldered figure clothed in a crisp white short-sleeved open-necked shirt and trim navy shorts, Laura found herself envying the way that he always managed to look so cool and unruffled—in sharp contrast to herself, the scruffy film crew and the heavily costumed actors, all visibly wilting in the steamy heat.

'When we arrived, I felt certain that it wouldn't be long before there was going to be a *real* mutiny,' she continued. 'But now that the writers have decided to lay off the booze, and everyone else has calmed down, the only problem you haven't yet solved seems to be the question of extra finance to complete the film.'

'I may be able to sort out some simple problems but I'm afraid I can't perform miracles!' he laughed, before ordering more drinks from a passing waiter.

Continuing to discuss various aspects of the troubled production, which, in her view at least, was destined to be a total flop at the box office, she was surprised when he suddenly announced that it was time they both had a break.

'A break...?' She frowned at him in puzzlement.

He shrugged his broad shoulders. 'Frankly, there's not much more we can do here—although Craig has asked me to let you stay on for another week, just in case any further problems should arise. Hey, relax!' he added with a grin as she groaned and pulled a face. 'I know looking after Craig isn't easy—but it's hardly a fate worse than death!'

'Maybe not, but it comes pretty close,' Laura grumbled, dreading having to cope with the neurotic, highly strung film star, who genuinely believed that he was totally irresistible to women. 'Do I really *have* to stay on here?'

'Yes, I'm afraid you do,' Jack told her firmly, explaining that he was returning to London after the weekend for an important meeting. However, with a few days in hand, he'd decided, he went on to tell her, to accept an invitation from the producer of the film, who'd arranged a trip to an archipelago of tiny atolls in the Pacific Ocean, only ninety minutes away by air from Tahiti.

'Quite frankly, Laura,' he added, 'for the past week we've been forced to listen to enough moaning and whining to last a lifetime! So it will do us both good to get away for a few days.'

'You mean... the invitation includes me as well?'

'Well, I was hardly planning to leave you behind,' he drawled sardonically. 'Unless, of course, you simply *hate* the idea of sitting beneath shady palm trees, gazing out over a blue lagoon—and savouring the total peace and quiet?'

'It sounds like heaven,' she agreed with a wistful sigh. 'But—'

'Good, that's settled,' he said firmly as he rose to his feet. 'I'm going to be tied up with business calls for the rest of this evening, but I've arranged for us to be collected from the hotel first thing tomorrow morning. By the way, don't forget to pack your bikini,' he added, gently brushing her cheek with his finger before turning to stride away.

Left alone on the terrace, Laura's mind was filled by a mass of confusing emotions as she gazed blindly out over the ocean, now barely visible in the gathering darkness. Back in London, frantically busy during working hours with the phone going non-stop, she normally had no trouble in stifling her feelings for Jack. But she wasn't at all sure that this weekend break was a good idea. Especially when merely the soft, warm touch of Jack's hand on her face could leave her feeling almost sick with hunger and desire.

It had, of course, been nothing more than a careless, friendly gesture. But there didn't seem to be anything she could do about the almost overwhelming, deep longing to find herself clasped within his strong embrace.

Desperately trying to pull herself together, Laura realised that she was undoubtedly guilty of overdramatising the situation. After all, she and Jack weren't likely to be alone on this trip. Sam, the producer, was a jovial and gregarious man who was almost bound to have asked several other actors and staff to join him. So allowing herself to get into a state about spending a weekend in Jack's company wasn't just silly—it was totally pathetic!

However, despite sternly lecturing herself on the folly of indulging in hopelessly romantic dreams, she slept badly that night. And when she descended to the hotel lobby the next morning it was to discover that her strong sense of apprehension and foreboding had been well founded, after all.

'The balloon has just gone up,' Jack announced as he led her towards a waiting taxi, explaining that the financial backers of the film had apparently run out of patience and were threatening to withdraw funding. With Sam and his assistants having to catch the first plane back to New York, in a desperate attempt to save the production, it now seemed that only Jack and Laura would be free to enjoy the weekend.

'But... but surely we can't just disappear like this?' she muttered nervously. 'Most of the cast will be out of their minds with worry, and—'

'Nonsense! There's absolutely nothing we can do about the situation,' Jack said as their taxi sped through the crowded, noisy streets of Papeete towards the airport. 'And I certainly don't intend to spend the next few days wet-nursing a bunch of grouchy, bad-tempered people— however sorry I might feel for them,' he added firmly, refusing to listen when she pointed out that their client,

Craig Jordan, wouldn't be at all happy with their departure from the unhappy scene.

'Craig is perfectly capable of looking after himself for a few days,' her employer retorted dismissively. 'And, since fate has clearly taken a hand in this affair, what I *now* have in mind certainly doesn't include a third party!' He paused for a moment before adding quietly, 'However, if you really don't feel like coming on this trip, Laura, then you only have to say so.'

There was no mistaking the glint in his grey eyes, the warm smile accompanying his words causing her to feel unexpectedly breathless, her heart pounding with a crazy mixture of soaring, wild excitement and nervous apprehension. Did 'what I have in mind' mean what she thought it did? Because, if so, she was going to have to take a very quick decision. Once she got on that plane with Jack, there would be no going back. Whatever the outcome, their relationship was never going to be the same again.

On the other hand, he was at least playing fair and giving her the chance to call the whole thing off. So, the safe, sensible decision would be to firmly and politely decline to accompany him on the trip—right? Unfortunately, it was proving difficult, if not downright impossible, to think clearly at the moment. It suddenly seemed as if he was sitting far too close, her mind and concentration distracted by the long, mahogany-brown legs almost touching her own, her nostrils filled with the strangely intoxicating, heady tang of his cologne.

Deciding to be sensible, Laura took a deep breath, fully intending to say that she'd prefer to remain in Tahiti. She was, therefore, considerably astounded to find herself agreeing that, yes...maybe a short break would be a good idea after all.

Totally unable to explain to herself, let alone to anyone else, why she should have agreed to such an emotionally insane invitation, it seemed to Laura as if she spent the rest of the day in a completely mindless daze.

Their hotel, on a tiny atoll fringed by totally deserted white sandy beaches and overlooking the crystal-clear waters of a dark blue lagoon, was far more breathtakingly beautiful than she could have ever imagined. However, she was aware only of the tall, dark man who had dominated her dreams for so long. Drowning helplessly in the gleaming depths of his slate-grey eyes as they dined alone on the candlelit terrace of the hotel, of which they appeared to be the only guests, she allowed herself to be led, like a sleepwalker, to the door of his room overlooking the lagoon.

'It's not too late to change your mind, Laura, if you think this isn't a good idea,' he said softly.

She gave a bemused shake of her head. 'No, I...er...I think I know what I'm doing...' she murmured, totally caught up in the magic of the moment.

'I'm glad someone has their feet on the ground, because I certainly haven't,' he muttered thickly under his breath, drawing her into his room and kicking the door closed behind them. 'God knows, I've tried to be sensible—but I simply can't seem to help myself.'

'I don't understand...' she whispered helplessly as he drew her close to his tall, rangy figure.

'Surely you must have guessed that I've been absolutely crazy about you for the past year?' The thick, husky tone of his low voice seemed to echo in her ears. 'I'll never know how I've managed to keep my hands off you for so long...' he breathed as his arms closed tightly about her slim frame, his mouth possessing her lips in a kiss of passionate intensity.

With her mind and body seized by a raging tide of sexual excitement and desire, she ardently welcomed the fierce, determined possession by his lips and body. Beside the clamouring demand of their mutual desire, all sense of caution or moral precepts seemed totally unimportant and unreal.

Throughout that long night, it seemed to Laura as if she'd become completely lost to all sense of time and place. She was only aware of a compulsive need to respond to the soft, long, sweeping caress of his fingers, purring and glowing with rapture as she unashamedly offered her nude body to his eyes and hands, her own senses delighting in the firm texture of his flesh and the hard muscles of the arms fiercely pulling her towards him.

Beneath the mastery of his touch, it seemed as though she had become a wanton creature, her nostrils savouring his musky, masculine scent, her lips tasting the salty fragrance of his skin, until overwhelming desire yet again claimed them both, a frenzied need not merely to be possessed, but to be totally consumed and fulfilled, the intensity of their lovemaking causing her to cry out loud with joy and overwhelming happiness.

Now, as she looked back on those two, brief days which they'd spent together, scarcely leaving the small cottage at their hotel—other than to wander hand in hand into the calm blue waters of the lagoon, or stroll along the fine, powdery white sand of deserted beaches—Laura found herself wondering if, in reality, it had all been a dream. With her being so madly in love with Jack, maybe her over-fertile imagination really had, somehow, conjured up that blissful, halcyon time of enchantment and rapture.

Because it was the only explanation which appeared to make any sense of what had happened less than twenty-four hours after her return to London. Even now, over three weeks later, she could still almost feel her skin crawling with the humiliation of Jack's cool, ruthless rejection—a crushing blow from which she was finding it well-nigh impossible to recover.

Slipping on a bathrobe and winding a towel about her damp hair, she wandered disconsolately out of the bathroom, deciding to drown her sorrows in a cool drink. But, just as she was making her way to the kitchen, she heard a ring on the doorbell.

Grumbling under her breath at the repeated, loud buzz of the bell, Laura tightened the belt of her towelling gown and went to open the door.

'What...what on earth are *you* doing here?' she gasped, suddenly feeling quite sick as she gazed through the few inches of open door, which still had its chain firmly in place.

'To see you, of course,' Jack retorted, his lips tightening as the pale-faced girl continued to stare at him with shocked, glazed eyes. 'Come on, Laura,' he added with ill-concealed impatience. 'Undo the chain and let me in.'

After a moment's hesitation, she gave a helpless shrug and did as he asked, stepping back in silence and allowing him to walk past her into the apartment.

'I still can't think what you're doing here,' she muttered, finding her voice at last as she reluctantly followed him into the sitting room. 'In fact, you're just about the *last* person I expected to see.'

'I've been in the United States for the past few weeks. In fact, I've come here straight from the airport,' he said, brushing a tired hand through his thick, dark hair. 'As I suspected when we were in Tahiti, it now looks as if the film's financial problems have just about scuppered *Mutiny on the Bounty.*'

'So, what else is new?' she retorted caustically. 'Anyone with half an eye could see that the film was going to be a Grade A flop.'

He shrugged. 'Flop or not, I had to make sure that the financial backers honoured Craig's contract. However, the time I spent in America wasn't entirely wasted, because I've now decided to open an office in New York.'

'Yes, well, I'm sure that's all very interesting,' she snapped, nervously tightening the belt of her robe and deeply resenting the way his tall figure, formally elegant in a dark suit, seemed to dominate even the large sitting room.

'However, *just* in case you've forgotten,' she continued grimly, 'you sacked me some three weeks ago. So your current business plans have absolutely nothing to do with me. Right?'

'Wrong,' he retorted curtly, before giving an impatient sigh at the cold, stony expression on her face. 'Relax—I haven't come here to quarrel with you, Laura. So why don't you come down off your high horse and give me a cup of coffee?'

'A cup of coffee?' she echoed blankly, completely astounded by the sheer nerve of the awful man. Did he really imagine that he could just casually swan back into her life, as if nothing had happened?

'I'm feeling so jet-lagged that either coffee, tea or a stiff drink would be equally welcome,' he explained with a weary shrug of his broad shoulders.

'Quite frankly, Jack,' she retorted grimly, 'the *only* thing I feel like giving you is a very hard thump on the nose!'

He gave a short bark of wry laughter. 'That's what I love about you, darling—you're all heart!' he murmured, his lips curving into such a warm, infectious grin that her pulse seemed to miss a beat and she felt quite dizzy for a moment. 'However, I would be grateful if you'd put that thump on hold for a while—because not only am I practically dying of thirst, but we obviously need to have a long talk.'

Five minutes later, and furious with herself for being so weak and feeble, Laura was swearing grimly under her breath as she removed two wineglasses from a kitchen cupboard, before moving over to explore the contents of the fridge.

What on earth was wrong with her? Why was she in here, meekly getting the beastly man his cold drink, when she *should* have given him a hefty kick in the shins and told him to get lost? Because she was spineless—that was why! she told herself glumly.

And what about all that good advice which she'd been giving herself over the past three weeks, and which now seemed to have been a complete waste of time? If all it took to reduce her stomach to rubble was a charming smile and a disturbing gleam in the slate-grey, heavy-lidded eyes of her ex-employer—currently making himself comfortable in her sitting room—it looked as if she was in deep, *deep* trouble.

On the other hand...tossing Jack out on his ear wasn't really a viable course of action, she consoled herself miserably. For one thing, he was far taller and heavier than she was. And, if she was really honest, she didn't entirely loathe the idea of what he'd referred to as 'a long talk'. Especially as she intended to do all the talking! I'll tell him his fortune, she promised herself grimly. By the time I've finished with that Casanova, he'll *definitely* wish that he'd stayed celibate all his life!

'I'm afraid the cupboard is rather bare at the moment. All I could find in the fridge was a bottle of white wine,' she told him, carrying a tray through into the sitting room.

'That's fine,' he murmured, rising from the long, comfortable sofa to take the glass from her hand. 'I didn't realise that you had such a glamorous apartment,' he added, gazing up at the high lofty ceilings and the enormous windows draped in yards of billowing white muslin, through which could be seen a panoramic view of the rooftops of Soho. 'Have you been here for some time?'

'Unfortunately, no—and I won't be able to remain here for much longer, either.'

'Why ever not?'

'Because the rat for whom I used to work threw me out of my job,' she told him bitterly. 'And, since the said rat has also failed to honour his promise of a handsome settlement, I now can't afford to keep up the mortgage payments. All of which means that this apartment will be up for sale probably as of next week.

However,' she added caustically, 'since *you* seem to like it so much, maybe you'd like to buy it for yourself?'

'Oh, God—I'm sorry.' He grimaced, brushing a hand roughly through his dark hair. 'I've been so busy that I completely forgot... However, I promise to see that you get a large cheque first thing in the morning.'

She shrugged her slim shoulders. 'That's nice, but it doesn't alter the fact that without a job I've got no real hope of being able to stay here. Have you got an answer to that small problem as well?'

'Yes, as it happens, I think I have,' he drawled. 'But, before we get around to discussing the position I have in mind, we need to have a cool, calm and sensible discussion about what has happened in the past. However, that doesn't seem likely at the moment,' he added drily, his eyes glinting with amusement. 'Not if you're going to remain standing on the other side of the room, bearing a strong resemblance to Joan of Arc at the stake!'

'At least Joan had got her priorities straight,' Laura lashed back angrily. 'She knew a slimy Englishman when she saw one!'

'Why don't you come and sit down over here and give me a chance to set the record straight?' he drawled smoothly, clearly refusing to be provoked into a quarrel. 'Surely it ought to be possible for the two of us to try to act like adult human beings?'

It all sounded very reasonable, but Laura wasn't fooled by his mild, smooth tone of voice. Not for one minute! If that ruthless operator Jack Wilder thought that he was going to be able to sweet-talk her into putting up with any more of his nonsense, he definitely had another think coming! And it was no good him flashing that engagingly warm, oh, so charming smile in her direction, either. The man was nothing but a two-timing, heartless swine, and she certainly had no intention of forgetting that fact.

Still . . . well, he *had* briefly mentioned that he might have a position in mind for her. It was awful to be so mercenary, of course, but with her finances in such dire straits maybe she ought to at least listen to what he had to say?

'OK,' she sighed. 'I'll give you the opportunity to set the record straight. But you'll have to cool your heels for a moment while I remove this wet towel from my head.'

Escaping to the sanctuary of her bedroom, and firmly closing the door behind her, Laura knew that she really didn't have enough time to change out of her towelling robe. And she certainly had no intention of letting Jack think that she was prepared to make an effort just for his sake. All the same, she'd have to do *something*, she realised as she gazed at her reflection in the mirror, wincing with dismay at the sight of her pale, chalky-white face and bedraggled, wet auburn hair.

However, there was no law that said she couldn't put on some make-up. And, in fact, now she came to think about it, the American Indians had been absolutely right. Because, when going into battle, a girl definitely needed some war paint, she told herself grimly, swiftly applying colour to her cheeks and trying to control the slim lipstick in her nervous, shaking hand as she brushed a soft pink over her trembling lips.

Well, you certainly look a whole lot better. Maybe you can manage to fool him, if not yourself, Laura silently told her reflection in the dressing-table mirror, only too conscious, as she straightened her gown and tightened the belt, that Jack's sheer, physical presence was having an alarming effect on her emotions.

Why couldn't he just go away and leave her alone? It hadn't been easy, but she'd managed to survive the past three weeks. Mainly buoyed up by her anger and resentment, of course. But at least that had been better than nothing. But now Jack had suddenly materialised—like the wicked demon in a pantomime, trailing green smoke and casting his wicked spell over her once again—and he was obviously quite confident of persuading her that, despite his rotten behaviour, he was really a wonderful human being after all.

Relax! All you have to do is to hear him out—and then show him the door, she mouthed silently at herself in the mirror. Unfortunately, the green eyes gazing back at her were not half as confident as her words. They clearly had severe doubts and dire misgivings about her ability to cope with such an upsetting, emotionally fraught situation.

CHAPTER THREE

DESPITE summoning up all the courage at her command, Laura was still miserably aware of a sick, nervous lump in her stomach as she forced herself to return to the sitting room. Thus, after resolutely bracing herself to face an emotional confrontation, it was maddening to discover the long-legged figure of her ex-employer now lying flat out on her cream leather sofa—fast asleep.

He certainly believed in making himself comfortable, she thought sourly, noting that he'd thrown his jacket and tie onto one chair and his briefcase onto another. She'd spent all day cleaning and polishing up her apartment, and yet, less than half an hour after his arrival, the place was already looking a mess!

Jet lag or no jet lag, there was no way she was going to put up with any of his nonsense, Laura told herself grimly, ruthlessly crushing her first instinctive feelings of concern as she stood at the end of the couch, viewing the lines of exhaustion and fatigue etched on Jack's tanned features. She didn't need reminding that a leopard never changes his spots. So it was a complete waste of time feeling sorry for the rotten man.

He might have had a long, tiring flight, but, since he regularly flew back and forth across the Atlantic, there were no prizes for guessing that he'd also been out on the town in New York last night with one of his many glamorous girlfriends. Well, good luck to her—because she'd soon find out that she was merely one in a long, *long* line of completely bamboozled, foolish women.

'You're looking a bit grim.'

Jack's deep voice cut through her distracted thoughts like a dash of icy cold water. Staring down at his supine figure, she noticed that, despite his lazily yawning and stretching his tall frame, the grey eyes regarding her from beneath their heavy lids were glinting with a sharpness and clarity which did absolutely nothing for her peace of mind.

'Well, how do you expect me to look? My present life isn't exactly a bed of roses, you know,' she retorted bluntly.

'Yes, I'm sorry that I've caused you so much trouble and worry.' He frowned. 'I had no idea...'

'OK, OK, we've already been over that aspect of my current problems.' She waved her hand dismissively in the air, well aware that her present situation was partly her own fault. Laura knew that if she'd had any sense she would have been more prudent, carefully saving part of her large salary for *just* such a rainy day. However, that wasn't something she was prepared to admit publicly—and certainly not to her ex-employer, now lying at his ease on the pale leather couch and looking as if he hadn't a care in the world.

'Quite frankly, I'm not interested in listening to any of your usual hearts and flowers nonsense,' she continued bleakly. 'So can we please get down to the nitty-gritty of *exactly* what you're doing in my apartment?'

Jack's lips had tightened ominously at her caustic reference to his well-known charm and lifestyle. But it was only a moment or two before he clearly had himself well under control once again.

'I've already told you to relax, sweetheart,' he drawled, deciding to ignore the obvious rage and fury of the girl now standing at the end of the sofa with her hands on her hips and glaring down at him with such stormy green eyes. In his experience, women definitely did *not* want to be told that they looked far more beautiful when they were angry. So, for the moment, perhaps it would be as well to tread carefully, and concentrate on resolving some of their problems?

'I came here today to see you,' he continued, 'with the sole purpose of bringing you tidings of comfort and joy.'

She gave a snort of cynical disbelief. 'That'll be the day!'

' "O ye of little faith"!' he murmured, his lips curving into a broad grin of sardonic amusement.

Maybe it was that arrogant, supremely confident smile that finally pushed her over the edge? Mulling over the unfortunate episode later, Laura would realise that losing her temper with the awful man had not been a good idea. But, suddenly consumed with blind rage at his damned condescension—*and* the fact that he seemed to be using her home to recover from a night out on the tiles!—she hadn't given a thought to the consequences.

'Don't you dare quote the Bible at me, you...you two-timing Casanova!' she stormed. 'And my apartment is definitely *not* a rest-home for tired old theatrical agents,' she added furiously, bending down to push his feet off the sofa.

The next few seconds seemed to whiz by in a blur. One moment she was leaning down over the arm of the couch, and then—in what seemed like the twinkling of an eye—she found herself being pulled roughly forward, almost flying through the air, before finding herself lying sprawled on top of Jack's long, hard body.

'For heaven's sake!' she gasped, lying winded and dazed for a moment. Then panic set in as she felt his arms closing about her. 'What ... what on earth do you think you're doing?'

'I don't like being referred to as either "old" or "tired". Nor do I care to be shouted at by hoity-toity females!' he drawled with silky menace, although there was a faint smile on the face only inches away from her own.

'I can't think why you've suddenly become so choosy. Everyone knows you just *love* chatting up your difficult female clients,' she retorted breathlessly, frantically trying to wriggle free from the arms now ominously tightening about her like bands of steel.

'Ah, but you're talking about work. While this ...' he gave a low, sensual laugh '...this definitely comes under the heading of play!'

'Not for me, it doesn't!' she panted, furious at finding herself so firmly trapped in his embrace and desperately trying to ignore the effect that his hard, muscular body was having on her own, trembling figure.

Jack raised his head, the piercing grey eyes studying her flushed features for a brief moment. 'Liar!' he taunted, his broad shoulders shaking with wry amusement as he leaned back on the cushions once more.

'OK, Jack—you've made your point. Now, *please* let me go!' she begged huskily.

'No...no, I don't think so. I'm rather enjoying myself at the moment,' he murmured softly. 'On the other hand, I can't help thinking that we'd both be more comfortable if our positions were reversed.'

'No!' she shrieked. But he was already putting his words into action. A second later, she found herself lying on her back, trapped against the rear of the sofa on one side, with Jack's broad-shouldered figure firmly blocking her escape on the other.

'I'm not putting up with this sort of nonsense!' she declared breathlessly as she struggled to sit up, grimly tugging at part of her long robe which had become caught beneath his body. 'Let me go!'

'Not just at the moment...' he murmured, leaning forward to trap her beneath him, raising his hand to brush a stray lock of hair from her face before tucking it gently behind her ear.

'Are you deaf? I *said* that I want you to let me go,' she hissed, doing her best to ignore the swirling mass of emotions racing through her veins at his soft touch.

Completely ignoring her protests, he slowly and deliberately wound his fingers through her damp hair. 'The past few weeks have been hell without you, Laura,' he muttered. 'I hadn't realised just how much I need you by my side.'

Laura froze, all her senses screaming a warning as she registered the thick, husky note in his voice and the disturbing gleam in the flint-grey eyes gazing so intently down into hers. 'Well, that's just your tough luck!' she retorted, determined to defy this man to the bitter end.

'So you didn't miss me—not for one minute?'

'Are you kidding? Absolutely *not*!'

'Oh, dear...oh, dear,' he mocked softly. 'Didn't your mother teach you not to tell fibs?'

She *must* get out of this situation—and as quickly as possible. But, despite frantically struggling to escape, she realised it was too late as he pulled her closer, his fingers tightening in her hair to hold her firmly imprisoned against him.

'I'm *not* lying!' she protested untruthfully, bitterly aware of her body's instinctive response to the hard, firm warmth of the figure pressed so closely to her own. 'Believe me—a day away from you is like a . . . a month in the country!'

'Bitch!' He sounded half-angry, half-amused, as if her continuing defiance was causing him some ironic enjoyment. 'Why keep on trying to fool yourself? You know that you're crazy about me!'

'You're so damn sure of yourself, aren't you?' she ground out huskily.

'I'm *very* sure about you!' he agreed in a low, throbbing whisper as his dark head came slowly and inexorably down towards her.

Hot shivers of erotic excitement seemed to grip her stomach as she trembled against him, certain that he must be able to hear the frantic, rapid pounding of her heart beating in close unison with his own.

'Please...no...!' she gasped helplessly as his lips softly possessed hers, her protest becoming an inaudible moan as she found herself surrendering to the beguiling sweetness of his kiss.

Still holding her trapped firmly beneath him, his hand left her hair, sliding slowly down to slip inside her robe, finding the warm softness of her naked breast, and his fingers brushed over the hard, swollen peak, causing a fierce tremor of pleasure to rage through her trembling body.

'Sweetheart . . .!' She barely heard the muffled groan as his mouth left hers and trailed down over the long curve of her throat, his lips pressing to the scented hollow at its base. He murmured husky words of pleasure as his hands moved enticingly over her bare flesh, moulding her soft body even closer to his.

Because she was completely enmeshed in a feverish, dizzy haze of burning excitement, it was some time before the loud ringing of the doorbell managed to penetrate the sensual mist of desire which had filled her mind to the exclusion of all else.

Oh, *no*! She had to stop this—*right now*! It wasn't just the fact that there was obviously someone at her front door. It was also obvious that she must have completely lost her marbles! What on earth had possessed her to surrender so easily to Jack Wilder's lethal charm? How *could* she have forgotten that her life had just been entirely ruined by this wicked man?

'Forget it!' he muttered thickly as she began struggling violently in his arms.

But, for Laura, the subtly woven dark enchantment, which had held her so firmly trapped within its spell, was now completely shattered. With a determined effort, she finally managed to struggle free of his relaxed embrace, frantically scrambling off the sofa before his long arms could trap her once again.

The bell had stopped ringing. Whoever it was had obviously given up, but the damage was done. It was just as well that she *was* going to sell this apartment, she thought miserably, her shaking hands all fingers and thumbs as she tried to pull the edges of her dishevelled gown tightly together. Because the sooner she got out of here, placing herself well beyond the reach of this totally lethal, dangerous man, the better. Maybe emigrating to Australia might be a good idea? If the TV soaps they regularly turned out were anything to go by, there was obviously a thriving theatrical life to be found on the other side of the world.

But who was she kidding? Even placing over ten thousand miles between herself and Jack wouldn't make an ounce of difference to the plain, unadulterated fact that she was still madly in love with him. Oh, help! *What on earth was she going to do?*

Rising leisurely from the sofa, Jack stared intently over at the clearly unhappy, hunched figure of the girl sitting huddled in a large armchair. And then he moved smoothly over the kelim rugs covering the polished oak floor towards the kitchen.

'Here—this will make you feel better.'

'I doubt it,' she mumbled as Jack returned, placing a glass of cool white wine in her hands before carrying his own drink over to one of the large arched windows.

'Well, if alcohol doesn't do the trick, then possibly the offer of a job may succeed in doing so.'

'What job?' she muttered, still trying to combat the shame and humiliation of having just clearly demonstrated that she was a complete pushover, spineless, nothing but soft putty in his experienced hands.

Jack remained standing silently by the window for a moment, before turning around to face her.

'I told you, when I arrived here earlier this afternoon, that I wanted to set the record straight. It's important that you understand it was simply *because* of our changed relationship that you had to leave my firm. I wasn't lying or making excuses that day in my office. I can promise you that I have never known a case of two people working together in an office and subsequently falling in love with one another whose relationship didn't end in anything but trouble.

'Yes, I know.' He raised a hand as she opened her mouth to protest. 'There's always going to be an exception, of course. But I have yet to come across even one happy outcome to a work-orientated love affair.'

He turned back to the window. 'My own marriage is a case in point. I'm not saying that Melissa and I would still be married if she hadn't worked in the office when I first started up the business and couldn't afford to hire a first-class secretary. Because, in fact, her subsequent marital history of picking up and discarding husbands would seem to prove that I was just unlucky,' he added with a rueful shrug of his broad shoulders.

'However, that was a long time ago,' he continued. 'And, while I'm a lot older and wiser now, of course, I have absolutely *no* intention of ever making that mistake again. Which is why—' he turned back to face her '—I felt I had to act as quickly and ruthlessly as I did. If I cared about you—and I can assure you that I do—I had to make sure that our new relationship was placed on a different footing. One that was well away from the trials and tribulations of the workplace. Surely you can see that what I'm saying makes sense?'

'Well, yes...maybe...' She shrugged helplessly. 'But you *still* don't seem to understand. I really loved my job—and truly believed that I was good at it. And then you...you suddenly pulled the rug out from beneath my feet. I'm sorry for all those horrid things I said in the office that day,' she added with a sigh. 'But it was such a terrible shock! Especially after...after that time we'd spent together in the South Pacific.'

'It was very important to me too,' he assured her quietly.

'Well, how on earth was I supposed to know that?' she flashed back, with some of her old belligerence.

'Oh, come on, Laura!' He gave another of his low, sensual laughs that practically made her toes curl, her stomach clenching in sudden tension at the unmistakable message reflected in his glinting grey eyes. 'I thought I'd demonstrated—quite clearly!—exactly how I felt about you.'

'Which is precisely why I simply couldn't *believe* what was happening to me when I returned from Tahiti! Or that you were capable of being so cruel—so...so heartless,' she retorted, hunting in the pockets of her gown for a handkerchief to blow her nose, and bitterly ashamed of the weak tears filling her eyes and threatening to fall any minute.

'I mean...it's all very well to try and sweet-talk your way out of it now,' she continued, determined not only to make him understand what he'd done, but also to keep her weak, feeble heart under control, 'but every scrap of evidence pointed to the fact that I was being ruthlessly dumped—both from my job and your life. To put it crudely, that you regarded me as nothing more than another notch on your bedpost!'

His dark brows drew together in a sharp frown. 'You're quite right—that statement *is* crude,' he snapped tersely. 'It also happens to be totally false.'

She gave a helpless shrug. 'I'd like to believe that's true. But, quite frankly, Jack, you've got a really rotten reputation. And, after what's happened, I still wouldn't trust you any further than I could throw you.'

He sighed, roughly brushing his long fingers through his thick, dark hair. 'I can assure you that my so-called ''reputation'' is mostly a figment of the newspaper gossip pages' and some people's overheated imaginations. As sensible adults, we both know that trust isn't something which is arrived at overnight. It's built up over a matter of time—and clearly there's nothing much I can do about that problem at the moment.

'However,' he added firmly, 'I never had any intention of ''dumping'' you, as you put it. We only had two short days and nights together. But I believed they were important, to both of us. And if we hadn't lost our tempers with one another—swiftly followed by your abrupt departure from my office—I would have had the opportunity to say that I very much wished and hoped to continue our...er...intimate relationship.'

Laura shook her head bemusedly. With his tall, dark figure standing only a few feet away across the room, she was having difficulty in concentrating on what was obviously one of the most important conversations of her life. It very much sounded as if Jack was virtually saying that she could either have him or her job but she couldn't have both. And maybe if she hadn't fallen so deeply in love with the man she might have had the strength to tell him to get out of here, right now.

But, since her whole being seemed to be throbbing in direct response to the strong, sensual masculinity projected by this overwhelmingly attractive man, her mind seemed to be saying one thing and her heart quite another.

'Um...' She gave a slight cough and cleared her throat, trying to think how she could best frame her next sentence. Because, while she certainly couldn't blame anyone but herself for those mad, reckless nights spent on the small Polynesian atoll, Laura knew that she was, basically, a very old-fashioned girl. So, while she wasn't expecting a romantic proposal of marriage, she did need to know exactly what Jack had meant when he'd referred to his interest in continuing their relationship.

However, she didn't have a chance to say anything further as he began talking about his recent trip to America.

'I think I've already mentioned the agency's new branch office in the States? Not only is the timing right for expansion, but it would certainly be a help for our American clients to have representation on the other side of the Atlantic.'

'That idea certainly makes sense,' she murmured.

'I'm glad to see that you approve of at least *one* of my actions!' He grinned. 'Anyway, while I was in New York, kicking my heels and waiting around for the business of Craig's money to be resolved, I had time to sort out the plans for the new office, and also to think about finding just the right sort of job for you. And I've now come up with something which I'm sure is going to suit us both down to the ground.'

'You mean...?' She frowned in puzzlement.

'It's a bit complicated, and beginning to look like the child's game of Pass the Parcel! However, since I want my offices in New York and London to be multinational, I've taken on two young agents from the States—one of whom was already working over here in England for Bill Chapman's voice-over business. And two of my staff in London are being promoted to the New York office, which will be run by a well-known American agent. So there's now a vacancy in...'

Wow! Laura thought breathlessly, barely listening to what else he was saying about the complicated plans for his new office. If Jack was putting her in the picture like this, it *must* mean that he was going to offer her a position in the new American office. Was it the job of her dreams—or what? she asked herself excitedly, her mind suddenly filled with entrancing visions of herself wheeling and dealing in the frenetic, exciting atmosphere of downtown New York.

'I...I simply don't know what to s-say...' she stuttered.

'There's no need to say anything.' Jack smiled at the flushed cheeks of the girl gazing at him with glazed eyes. 'However, I'm glad that you approve of my plans.'

'Oh, I do!' she agreed fervently. 'Have you...er...decided on exactly *who* you're sending to New York?' she asked, quickly deciding that this wasn't the moment to appear too pushy. It would be best if she left him to tell her the exciting news.

He nodded. 'I've decided to send James and Henry. They were delighted to hear about their transfer, of course, and I think they'll both make a definite contribution to the new business.'

As Jack continued to expand on his plans for the new office, his tall figure moving idly about the sitting room, pausing every now and then to admire either a picture or one of the pieces of blue and white china which she'd been slowly collecting over the years, Laura felt herself growing slowly numb. The initial excitement and euphoria of a few moments ago was now rapidly draining away. And, despite the warmth of the early summer evening, she suddenly felt desperately cold and very close to tears.

Thank God she'd kept her mouth shut—and hadn't made too much of a fool of herself, was one of the few clear thoughts to emerge from the almost total confusion in her mind. But, after a few moments, as she slowly pulled herself unsteadily together, her head began to feel as though it was swelling up like a balloon. One that was filled to overflowing with icy cold rage, and about to burst open at any moment.

'I ... I simply *refuse* to believe it!'

'What?' He spun around to face her. 'What don't you believe?'

'I can understand you sending James over to the States,' she grated hoarsely, desperately struggling for control. 'He's worked really hard, and deserves the promotion. But...but why send Henry—of all people? He's lazy, inefficient, desperately slow when there's a crisis, and...and was recently demoted to working as *my* assistant. In fact,' she added grimly through clenched teeth, 'the *only* possible reason I could see for you *not* giving him the sack was that his uncle is a well-known Hollywood producer!'

'Which is precisely why he's going to New York,' Jack agreed blandly. 'In setting up the new firm, I'm going to need all the help and contacts I can find. And, although I agree that Henry is fairly useless, his uncle is very keen for his nephew to do well in the agency business.'

'That...that's disgusting!'

He shrugged. 'You may well be right. But it's a rat race out there. And it's no good being too squeamish in our profession.'

'You speak for yourself!' she snapped. 'As far as I'm concerned, the trouble with a rat race is that even if you win you're still a rat.'

'Am I supposed to take that remark personally?'

'If the cap fits—wear it!' she retorted swiftly, no longer caring what she said or did. 'However, let's leave you

New York office aside for the moment. Because I'm still waiting with bated breath to hear all about this job which you've apparently arranged for me.'

He frowned at the heavy note of sarcasm in her voice. 'But I've just explained the whole damned set-up. Haven't you been listening to a thing I've said?'

'I think you'd better spell it out for me, in words of one syllable,' she retorted curtly.

He sighed with exasperation. 'Since I've taken on the young American who used to work for Bill Chapman's voice-over business, there's now a vacancy in that firm. As you know, it's a very specialised business, providing the voices to accompany TV and film commercials, as well as providing the dubbing for foreign films, et cetera. On top of which,' he added, 'it can be *very* lucrative.'

'So?' she demanded impatiently.

'So, when Bill was moaning about losing his assistant, and the fact that he's now having to look for a replacement, I immediately thought of you.'

'You did—*what*?'

'OK, OK, I'm not saying it's a particularly exciting firm to work for,' he conceded as she gave a shrill, high-pitched peal of hysterical laughter. 'But at least it *is* a job—and one in which you'll be able to earn a very high salary. However, as far as I'm concerned—' he gave her a warm smile '—its main attraction lies in the fact that we'll *still* be able to continue seeing a great deal of one another.'

Did he really think that she was a *total* idiot? Laura asked herself incredulously, almost unable to believe the evidence of her own ears. Because it now seemed as if this swine was intending to have his cake and eat it too! After all, what could be more convenient than to have a mistress working for another firm just around the corner from his own office? And one, moreover, whom he was clearly expecting to be always ready, willing and able to greet him with open arms, whenever he felt like a little night music! In fact, unless she was very much mistaken, it sounded as if this unbelievably awful man was dumping her—*yet again*!

Gazing with horrified eyes at his tall figure, now leaning nonchalantly against one of the large pillars in the room, Laura realised that she was quite right. Jack had obviously come here today intending to put into action his own private agenda—a nice, tidy arrangement, guaranteed to keep his ex-employee from causing too many waves in the small, intimate world of theatrical agents.

Well, he wasn't going to get away with it, she told herself grimly. Because there was a lot more at stake here than just her broken heart. No one...absolutely *no one* had the right to sack a hard-working, perfectly satisfactory employee without any prior notice. And, while she knew virtually nothing about the law regarding unfair dismissal, she was quite sure that she must have grounds to bring an action against her ex-employer.

'That's a very interesting proposition which you've just placed before me,' she said coldly, rising to her feet. 'Not exactly what *I'd* call "tidings of comfort and joy", of course, but definitely interesting! However, I'm sorry to have to tell you that it's one in which I have absolutely *no* interest at all. Especially when it also seems to involve being your convenient bit on the side.'

'Oh, come on, sweetheart! That's not what I have in mind at all,' he protested.

She snorted with derision. 'For heaven's sake, Jack—do you *really* think that I was born yesterday? We both know that Bill Chapman is a pompous little twit who spends most of his time in a bar around the corner from his office, leaving his assistant to run the business. No wonder the present guy is leaving to join your firm. *I* wouldn't even give Bill the time of day—let alone five minutes of my time! Oh, no...' Laura added grimly. 'I'm afraid you're going to have to do *much* better than that if you want to stop me taking you to court.'

'I don't know what you're talking about.'

'Now who's telling fibs?' she jeered, her lacerated emotions soothed by the sight of a faint flush on his high cheekbones. 'While I was having to listen to you bragging about your new office in New York—'

'I was doing nothing of the sort!'

'—I realised that if I *hadn't* been thrown out of your agency I'd have been the perfect candidate for one of the new posts,' she continued, ignoring his angry interjection. 'I also realised—and I can't think *why* it's taken me so long to wake up to the reality of the situation—that I must have a good claim for unfair dismissal over the way I was sacked. And don't even *try* and tell me that clever, ruthless Jack Wilder hasn't already talked over this little problem with his lawyers,' she added through gritted teeth. 'Because I'm now damn sure that he has!'

'You're talking complete nonsense,' he drawled smoothly. 'Of course I've seen my lawyers, who've been involved in the formation of my new American office. You'd hardly expect me not to take legal advice over such an important step?'

'Certainly not. However, having worked for you, I know *just* how thorough you can be—especially when it comes to reading the small print of actors' contracts. So it's virtually a certainty that you checked up on your legal position regarding my sudden dismissal. Just as I intend to do first thing tomorrow morning.'

'It's a waste of time trying to threaten me, Laura,' he informed her coldly. 'As far as I'm concerned this whole business is a farrago of complete nonsense.'

She shrugged. 'Well, you would say that, wouldn't you? However, the more I think about it, the more I realise just what a good case I've got. There's sexual harassment,' she began, counting off the items on her fingers, 'followed by unreasonable dismissal—and *serious* sex discrimination in giving dopey Henry the plum job in New York which should clearly have been offered to me. Quite honestly, Jack—' she gave him a tight, malicious smile '—I reckon I'm going to take you to the cleaners!'

'*Just* a minute!' he ground out angrily. 'What do you mean by "sexual harassment"?'

'I was still employed by you during our trip to Tahiti, right? I'm sure any court would take a dim view of a boss wickedly seducing his poor, innocent assistant, miles away from the comforts of her home and family.'

'Unless, of course, the wicked seducer claims that the so-called "innocent assistant" was, in fact, a raving nymphomaniac who seduced *him*!' Jack retorted swiftly.

'That . . . that's a damn lie!' she gasped.

'Prove it!' He gave a careless shrug, despite the glint of stormy menace in his hooded grey eyes.

'If you want to play these stupid sorts of games, Laura, it's entirely up to you,' he continued. 'However, if taken to court, I'll certainly claim that you were *more* than willing. Besides, we both know that I gave you several opportunities to change your mind about my wicked advances. Just as we *both* know that you're still crazy about me! So, I don't think a claim of sexual harassment is going to get you anywhere.'

'You can say what you like, but I still reckon that I've got a cast-iron case against you for unfair dismissal!' she retorted fiercely, determined not to let his vicious barbs get under her skin.

'Oh, come on, sweetheart!' he sighed, and shook his head. 'What *is* the point of us quarrelling like this? If you don't want to take the job with Bill Chapman, it's hardly the end of the world. The important thing is that you and I—'

'This row *isn't* about that rotten job—it's *you* I can't take any longer!' she lashed back angrily. 'It's obvious that finding me a dreary job in a voice-over agency is a good move on your part. It would certainly get me out of your hair, wouldn't it?' she added bitterly. 'But, if you think that I'm also taking on the job of your part-time mistress, you're very much mistaken!'

'I did *not* say that,' he retorted curtly.

'True—you didn't spell it out, but that's *exactly* what it sounded like to me. Or are we talking about a serious commitment to one another? Because it's about time you laid your cards on the table once and for all.'

'For heaven's sake, Laura!' He shook his head with exasperation. 'We hardly know one another. It's really far too early to—'

'Correction! We've worked closely together for a number of years. So I can't imagine there's much you don't know about me—or vice versa,' she retorted swiftly.

He stared at her incredulously for a moment, before giving a short, sharp bark of sardonic laughter. 'Are you seriously suggesting...? You aren't talking about marriage, surely?'

'Not necessarily,' she snapped. 'I'm talking about something you clearly don't understand: plain, boring, old-fashioned fidelity and commitment—either in or out of marriage. But that's a foreign country to you, right? Because what you've been *really* saying all along is: "If Laura is a good little girl, and minds her ps and qs, she may get to see the great Jack Wilder—when he isn't too busy seducing any other passing female who might catch his eye."'

Jack's lips tightened into a hard, thin line as her high-pitched, sing-song tone of voice seemed to echo around the room.

'For an intelligent woman you certainly can be incredibly stupid at times,' he grated angrily.

'Well, I'm sorry, but your idea of a relationship certainly isn't mine!'

'Rubbish!' he growled. 'You know that we care for one another.'

'That's where you're wrong!' she snapped, trembling with rage and fury at having been such a fool to have even let him inside her apartment. '*You* only care about Jack Wilder. So it's a case of thanks—but no, thanks,' she stormed. 'I'd rather lose this apartment and go hungry than accept the few miserable crumbs you're prepared to throw my way!' she added, marching determinedly towards the door. 'So get out—before I have you thrown out!'

'You must be stark raving mad—completely out of your mind,' he snarled, quickly catching hold of her arm as she tried to pass him, swiftly spinning her around to hold her hard up against his hard body. 'You *know* you're crazy about me.'

'I'm certainly crazy to have had anything to do with you,' she agreed bitterly. 'I should have known that such a two-timing, flaky human being wouldn't know what it means to *really* care about someone. Because caring means commitment—and you haven't the first idea of the meaning of the word!'

'Have you finished?' he growled savagely through tight lips, the skin beneath his tanned cheeks pale with rage and fury.

'I certainly have—now beat it!'

'Don't worry. I'm going! I should have known better than to fall for such an over-ambitious, work-obsessed virago, with hair the colour of carrots!' he sneered, before tossing her aside and striding quickly towards the front door.

'*Carrots*...? Are you colour-blind as well as being a two-timing bastard?' she yelled, quickly seizing a nearby cushion and throwing it after him as hard as she could. 'My hair is *auburn*—and don't you forget it!'

Still trembling with fury, she was astounded when, after opening the front door on his way out of her apartment, Jack returned to her sitting room only a few moments later.

'What *now*?' she demanded angrily.

'I found this left outside on your doorstep,' he retorted through clenched teeth, tossing her a huge, Cellophane-wrapped bouquet of flowers. 'So don't you *ever* again have the sheer, barefaced audacity to accuse *me* of being a two-timing bastard!'

But, before she could demand to know what on earth he was talking about, Jack had quickly spun around on his heel, his fast-disappearing figure swiftly followed by the sound of her front door being loudly slammed shut behind him.

A few minutes later, her normally soft lips set in a grim, angry line, Laura picked up the phone and began impatiently dialling a number.

How *dared* Jack open the small envelope pinned to the bouquet? Quite apart from anything else, it was none of his business *who* was sending her flowers, for heaven's sake! And how he could possibly take exception to the brief message—'I hope you'll reconsider your decision and agree to say yes to my proposal. Yours, Donald'— she had absolutely no idea.

However, this afternoon's confrontation had finally pushed her over the edge. If Jack Wilder thought that he could just walk all over her, he was going to find out that he was badly mistaken! Because not only was she now going to accept Donald Hunt's offer to set up her own theatrical agency, but she also had every intention of causing the *maximum* amount of trouble and grief for her rotten ex-employer!

CHAPTER FOUR

LAURA shook her head. 'No, I'm afraid that it *still* doesn't look right. Maybe it would be better if I sat with my back to the window?'

'Mmm...you could be right,' Susie agreed thoughtfully, both girls wincing at the sound of deep, audible groans from the removal men.

'Give us a break, darlin',' the foreman protested. 'You've already had us putting this flipping desk in more positions than the Kama Sutra!'

'I'm sorry,' Laura giggled. 'It's just that I can't quite—'

'Look—how about making us some tea or coffee in that high-tech kitchen of yours?' the foreman suggested, shepherding them firmly towards the door. 'And, while you're doing that, we'll see if we can't get things sorted out in here. Right?'

'That's the best idea I've heard all morning!' Susie laughed as she and Laura made their way down the corridor. 'Quite frankly, I could cheerfully murder someone for a cup of coffee!'

'While I'd happily sell my soul for a long, hot bath,' Laura admitted ruefully. 'I reckon that moving, whether it's to a new home or into a new office, is strictly for the birds!'

'High-tech' certainly seemed to be the perfect word to describe not only the kitchen but their new office suite as a whole, Laura told herself as she began filling the kettle, while Susie unpacked some cups and saucers. In fact, the sheer size of the three large and well-lit rooms, plus a luxurious bathroom and fully fitted kitchen—together with a collection of ultra-modern office desks and chairs—was still something she was having difficulty getting used to.

It was also making her feel extremely nervous about her new business venture. So many firms went into liquidation these days. Maybe she too would find herself facing bankruptcy—just like the previous occupant of these offices?

'The poor guy had hardly begun to unwrap the stuff before going spectacularly bust and high-tailing it off to South America,' Donald Hunt had explained, gesturing towards the smart, modern, Italian-designed furniture, when showing Laura and Susie around their new business premises. 'Luckily for you, as it turns out, he'd given me a year's rent in advance. So, have fun, girls!' Donald had added with a grin, before tossing them the keys and leaving Laura to survey her unknown future with nervous trepidation.

She was well aware that being driven by overwhelming rage and fury was not the best basis for the foundation of a new business. That sort of enterprise required, above all, a cool head and the ability to make objective decisions. On the other hand, maybe dashing in where angels might fear to tread had been the right approach after all. Because she'd been so busy over the hectic last few weeks that she really hadn't had time to think hard and long about her impetuous decision.

Donald Hunt had been amazingly generous. Calm and matter-of-fact, when she'd phoned him in an almost hysterical state, following the abrupt departure of Jack from her apartment, his cool and relaxed reception of the news that she'd changed her mind and would accept his backing for her own theatrical agency had done much to soothe her battered feelings. And in their subsequent meetings—which had also included Susie, whom she'd asked to join the new firm as her personal assistant—Donald had laid out the ground rules concerning his investment.

'You can have that office suite, rent-free, for the next twelve months,' he'd told them. 'And I'm also prepared to put in enough working capital to cover costs and your two salaries for the same amount of time. Which should enable you to get up and running.'

After mentioning the sum he had in mind, which had left Laura and Susie gasping at what they regarded as an amazing amount of money, Donald had also added a stern note of caution. 'I don't want you two girls to get *too* excited. Right here and now, twelve months might seem a long time. But you'll both find that it passes very quickly—especially if things start going well and you find yourselves rushed off your feet. You're also going to discover that I'm a hard task-master.'

However, Laura had been amused to note that his words of warning were accompanied by a warm smile in Susie's direction. Clearly Donald had taken a shine to the bubbly, petite blonde girl.

'While I'm not expecting you to repay me too fast or too soon,' he'd continued, 'I'll be keeping a regular eye on your accounts. That's just to make sure I'm not dealing with a lame-duck organisation, and that you're well on the way to making some serious money in the future.'

He'd also given them two strong pieces of advice. 'One: it's essential that you engage the services of a first-class bookkeeper, to come in regularly—say, once a week. Two: never skimp on the support staff. Because, if you try to save money by doing all the boring, mundane jobs, you won't have time to spend on the phone, or to get out and about meeting new contacts, which is essential if you're to succeed in this business.'

Both she and Susie had been grateful for his advice, and had laid their plans accordingly. Apart from the usual steps taken when setting up a business, Laura had been undecided as to what to call her new firm. After mulling over various ideas, she'd had a sudden flash of inspiration, which had sent her laughing all the way to Companies House to register the name she'd chosen. However, well aware that Susie was not likely to give it her wholehearted approval, Laura had been grateful that they were both so busy, thus enabling her to avoid any explanations until, she'd hoped, it would prove to be too late to alter her decision.

And they certainly had been busy! During the few short weeks between accepting Donald's offer and moving into their new business premises she'd spent long hours on the phone, contacting various casting directors and young, hot-shot theatre producers with whom she'd had a good working relationship in the past.

Unfortunately, Laura was only too well aware that in starting up a new agency she faced a difficult, chicken-and-egg situation. On the one hand, she must have the promise of exciting roles to offer her actors—while on the other she needed to have on her books a number of actors sufficiently talented to attract the interest of casting directors. It was a delicate balancing act, and there had been many times over the past few weeks when she'd wondered if she hadn't, in fact, bitten off far more than she could chew.

Ashamed of having suddenly fallen victim to stage-fright, and desperately trying to combat her misgivings about the large step she was taking, Laura had been comforted by her new assistant's brisk, no-nonsense approach to their business.

'Don't be ridiculous—*of course* you can do it! In fact, I'm quite certain that this firm is going to be a raving success,' Susie had told her, refusing to take any notice of her new employer's nagging doubts and uncertainty.

'We've both got masses of contacts in the business,' the other girl had reminded her. 'So it's my betting that it won't be long before we've got more work than we can handle. And for goodness' sake stop worrying about Jack Wilder's reaction,' she'd added firmly. 'I can't think why you seem to be so obsessed with our former employer. After all, he's such a big fish in the theatrical pond, why on earth should he be bothered about tiny minnows like us?'

Everything Susie had said made perfect sense. But, all the same, Laura was quite certain in her heart of hearts that Jack wasn't likely to be *at all* happy about her new venture. He would—quite rightly, of course—see her attempt to form an agency as a direct attack on him personally. And that was an aspect of their relationship which she couldn't, under any circumstances, discuss with Susie.

However, she'd done her level best to be honest and up front with her new assistant. After explaining that she and Jack had fallen out following a monumental row, the details of which she preferred to keep strictly private, Laura had been brutally frank about her feelings for her ex-employer.

'I don't want you to misunderstand the position,' she'd warned. 'Jack and I are now at daggers drawn with one another. In fact, it's probably true to say that we hate each other's guts! And, since you used to be *his* personal assistant, he might well resent the fact that you're now working for *me*. Once he discovers that I've set up my own agency—and in the same building as his office—I can virtually guarantee that he's going to be very angry indeed.'

But Susie had refused to listen to her words of caution. 'So you had a row and parted company. So what? It happens all the time, and especially in the theatrical business. Maybe it's something to do with looking after all those highly strung, temperamental film stars. Besides,' she'd added, 'I did contact Jack's office some months ago to see if there was any possibility of returning to work in the firm. But apparently he's now got a marvellous secretary, who has no intention of leaving her job.'

Laura nodded. 'While Betty and I didn't particularly like each other, I have to admit that she's the perfect, super-efficient and loyal-unto-death type of personal assistant.'

'Well, there you are.' Susie shrugged. 'If Jack couldn't offer me a job, it stands to reason that I was going to have to find one somewhere else. However, although I worked for him over a number of years and know *just* how hard and tough he can be at times, I refuse to believe that he's capable of being either mean or spiteful.'

Well, let's hope that Susie will prove to be right, Laura told herself now as she spooned instant coffee into the cups. In any case, it was pathetically feeble of her to be worrying about that ratfink Jack Wilder, who picked up and discarded women with the speed of light. She wouldn't be starting up her own business if he hadn't deliberately chosen to give her the sack. Not to mention his typically arrogant, male assumption that she'd still be willing to continue their relationship outside of business! Well, she'd certainly made her feelings clear about *that* crazy idea.

'Excuse me, darlin',' the foreman said, interrupting her unhappy thoughts, as he put his head around the door.

'We won't be a moment,' Laura told him hurriedly.

'Nah, it's not that. I just wanted to let you know that a smart geezer has just walked into the office, wanting to see whoever's in charge. And he don't look too happy, neither,' he added with a grimace.

'I can't think who...' She frowned. And, as Susie was gazing at her with an equally surprised and puzzled look on her face, Laura shrugged and followed the foreman back down the corridor.

Momentarily dazzled by a strong shaft of sunlight pouring in through the window of the largest office, Laura could only see the silhouette of a man outlined against the light. However, she immediately recognised the tall, dark figure, even before he swung around at the sound of her approach.

'My God—it really *is* true!' Jack ground out furiously. 'When Betty told me that a new firm had taken over these offices, and that she'd also caught sight of you entering the lift, I refused to believe her!'

'Betty always was a nasty bit of work. It's about time she learned to mind her own business,' Laura retorted breathlessly, desperately wishing that he hadn't caught her so unprepared. Dressed in jeans and a T-shirt, with virtually no make-up on her face and her hair in a mess, she hardly reflected the scenario she'd had in mind for their first meeting in her new offices.

'Kindly leave my secretary out of this!'

'That's no problem. Especially since I wouldn't dream of employing such a ghastly old snoop,' Laura countered grimly as the removal men scuttled hurriedly from the room.

'I refused to believe that it could possibly be *you*, of all people,' he continued, ignoring her sour comment. 'How can you *do* this to me? How can you be so unprincipled, so—?'

'Don't talk to me about *principles*!' she flashed back angrily. 'We both know that you don't have the first idea about the meaning of the word.'

'That's absolute nonsense—and you know it! I was totally honest and above board about the reasons why I had to ask you to leave. *I* didn't behave in a thoroughly devious, underhand manner, sneaking into this building and—'

'Hold it!' she snapped. 'You don't own me—or this building, for that matter. Since you never asked me to sign an exclusion contract which would have prevented me from working in the vicinity of your firm, I've a perfect right to start up a business anywhere I please.'

'Don't be ridiculous! What would *you* know about the mechanics of running a business?' he demanded with heavy sarcasm. 'And what is this so-called "business", anyway? Some pathetic computer dating service?' he added with a sneer, glancing around at the open boxes on the floor containing state-of-the-art office machinery. 'As far as I can see, your only qualifications are a university degree and some experience gained in the running of a theatrical agency.'

'Funny you should say that...' she murmured, suddenly filled with a feeling of mad exhilaration, and realising that the old saying was quite right. Revenge really *was* proving to be sweet—very sweet indeed. 'I came to exactly the same conclusion.'

'You... you don't mean...?'

'Mmm...' she cooed, giving him a wide, beaming, sickly sweet smile. 'And, since I owe you *so* much, I want you to be the first to know that I've decided to open my own theatrical agency.'

'Over my dead body!' he roared, his face as black as thunder.

'Oh, dear,' she muttered, desperately struggling not to laugh at the sight of her ex-employer practically dancing with rage. And then, deciding to give the knife another twist, she added, 'I thought you'd be pleased. Especially since I'll still be able to look after some of your old clients.'

'What do you mean by my "old" clients?' he ground out savagely, striding menacingly towards her. 'If I catch you trying to poach any of my actors, I... I'll have you in court so fast your feet won't touch the ground. And that's not a threat—it's a *promise*!' he added grimly, placing his hands firmly on her shoulders.

Raising her chin defiantly, and just about to tell him to get lost, she barely had time to even gasp in alarm as she found herself being pulled roughly up against his tall figure, her soft breasts crushed against his hard, muscular chest. Firmly pinning her against him with one large hand, and burying the other in her hair, Jack ruthlessly tugged her head back, tilting her face up towards him.

'I don't know what you think you're doing,' he growled with grim, silky menace, 'but I can tell you that this nonsense has got to stop, *right now*! If you think that I'm prepared to have an ex-employee starting up a business directly beneath my own office, you must be completely off your trolley!'

With those steely, granite-like eyes boring into her, it seemed as though her brain was being probed by lethal, laser-sharp skewers. Clasped so tightly in his arms, she was aware of the angry, hectic flush beneath the tanned skin covering his high cheekbones and formidable jaw, and her eyes were drawn helplessly to the cruel, sensual curve of his lips.

'You...you can't stop me!' she cried breathlessly, desperately trying to ignore the instinctive, quivering response of her traitorous body to the long, muscular thighs pressed so closely to her own.

It was always the same, she thought with despair. Every time she came anywhere near him, it seemed as though she was completely helpless, totally unable to prevent the white-hot flare of erotic attraction from scorching through her trembling limbs and destroying all her hard-fought, carefully erected defences against this man's fatal attraction.

'Let me go!' she croaked, frantically striving to escape his iron grip. 'There's nothing you can do to stop me operating from this office, and...and if you can't take the heat,' she added defiantly, 'then you'd better keep out of the kitchen!'

To her surprise, he merely responded to her provocative words with a low, rasping laugh, gazing fixedly down into her green eyes as some of the anger slowly drained from his face.

'All right, *sweetheart*!' he hissed menacingly. 'If that's the way you want to play it, then you'll just have to face the consequences!'

She'd barely managed to assimilate the dangerous glitter in his stormy grey eyes before his mouth came crushing down like a weapon against her lips, leaving her completely stunned, the relentless pressure almost paralysing in its intensity. Hardly able to breathe, and struggling against the arms which had tightened about her like bands of steel, she was aware of a treacherous warmth invading her limbs beneath the punishing assault which burned and demanded her submission.

Gradually and almost imperceptibly the cruel, ruthless pressure began to ease, his lips becoming warm and persuasive as they subtly coaxed and teased away all resistance. The hands which had been holding her so tightly now began to slowly slip-slide down over her soft curves, pressing her ever closer to his taut, muscular frame, so that Laura finally realised, from the hard arousal of his own body, that Jack was also a victim of the same deadly enchantment now winding its evil tentacles about their two still figures.

And then, with shocking suddenness, she found herself released from her torment. She lay limply in his arms like a rag doll, and it was some moments before she was able to get a grip on reality. With the limited mental energy at her command, Laura concentrated on trying to pull herself together, desperately striving to remain standing on legs which felt as though they were made of jelly, and likely to collapse at any moment. Which was why it took her some time to understand why Jack was cursing so violently under his breath.

Her dazed eyes slowly following his gaze, she was shattered to see Susie and the removal men standing frozen in the doorway. It was clear from their stunned expressions and, alas, the wide grin on two of the men's faces that they'd had a superb ringside view of all that had been taking place in her office.

Her cheeks flaming with mortification and shame, Laura desperately tried to think of something to say, some explanation which would enable her to emerge from this humiliating situation with at least her dignity intact. But unfortunately the task seemed completely beyond her.

Susie appeared to be the first to recover her wits. But the girl's evident intention of leaving the room as quickly as possible was foiled by the wide, burly figures of the removal men jammed in the doorway. Cringing at the obvious embarrassment on her assistant's face, Laura was nonetheless still feeling too stunned to say or do anything. However, it seemed that Jack had no such problem.

'Get the hell out of here—right this minute!' he rasped savagely. 'No, not you, Susie,' he snapped, frowning with irritation at the general mêlée as the men bumped into one another in their evident haste to leave the room. 'I definitely want to have a word with *you*!'

'No...I really don't think that I ought to get involved...'

'Too bad! You should have thought of that before having anything to do with this totally crazy, damn stupid enterprise of Laura's,' he growled, jabbing an accusing finger at the petite blonde girl still vainly trying to force her way past the bodies stuck in the doorway. 'You...you *traitor*!'

'Who? Me?' Susie squeaked, spinning around to stare at him with astonishment. 'What on earth do you mean?'

He gave a harsh bark of sardonic laughter. 'Don't play the innocent with me! Because if you're now working for this...this carrot-haired harpy—'

'Now *just* a minute!' Laura yelled, finding her voice at last.

'—you must need your head examined!' he ground out, completely ignoring both Laura's fury and her clumsy, unsuccessful attempt to land a hard kick on his shins.

'There's nothing wrong with *my* head—and I'm certainly no traitor!' Susie retorted hotly. 'I did try to return to work for your agency some months ago, but I was quite clearly told that you had no vacancies. So what was I supposed to do?' she demanded. 'Just stay at home and completely forget about working for anyone else? From the way you're going on, anyone would think that I'm committing some sort of crime.'

'Well, you've certainly made a great mistake in coming here to work for *her*,' he grated through clenched teeth, turning away from Susie to throw a glance of pure, undiluted hatred at the girl who'd been so firmly clasped in his arms only a few moments ago.

'If I do nothing else in this life, Laura, I'm going to make absolutely sure that your firm goes to the wall— and as quickly as possible,' he thundered, noting with satisfaction her pale, chalky-white face and trembling figure. 'By the time I've finished with you, you're going to wish that you'd never been born! And when—' He broke off as Susie gave a peal of scornful laughter.

'Really, Jack—this is all too silly for words!' she exclaimed. 'Why don't we just calm down and try to act like reasonable human beings?'

'When I want *your* advice I'll ask for it!'

'Well, that's tough, because I'm going to give it to you anyway,' she retorted, clearly refusing to be intimidated by the brooding menace of his tall, dark figure. 'Sure, you can go ahead and try and blacklist us—or whatever nasty scheme you have in mind. But what's it going to achieve? After all,' she added with a shrug, 'the first question anyone is going to ask is why Jack Wilder—owner of one of the most successful and prestigious theatrical agencies in London—should be *so* worried about such a very small, one-man band like this new firm.'

After pausing for a moment to let her words sink in, Susie continued, 'If *I* was a casting director, for instance, I might begin to wonder if perhaps you were beginning to lose your grip. And as for your clients... Well, we all know just how neurotic and fickle some actors can be. Especially if they suspect you're spending more time trying to put another firm out of business than concentrating on their own precious careers.' She shrugged. 'In fact, they might well decide they'd be better off leaving WHAM and joining the firm which is apparently giving you such a hard time.

'You've got a good point there, Susie.' Laura nodded in agreement. 'Most actors hate to feel that they might not be on the winning team.'

'Oh, *shut up*!' Jack turned to growl at her, before Susie once more claimed his attention.

'Surely your best course of action is to try and forget everything that's happened here today,' she pleaded with the man who was still clearly rigid with fury. 'I'm sure your desk is piled high with some really exciting, mega-dollar contracts and deals. So why waste your valuable time fighting a small, two-bit firm which hasn't even got off the ground?'

Jack stared grimly at the two women for a moment. 'I may well be in danger of "losing my grip" but I'm still *quite* capable of knowing when I've been outma-noeuvred!' he told them bitterly, before giving a heavy sigh of exasperation and striding grimly out of the room.

'*Phew*...!' Susie breathed with relief. 'There but for the grace of God—goes God!' she added, flinching at the sound of a loud bang as the front door of the office suite was slammed shut behind Jack's departing figure.

'I'm sorry...' Laura muttered huskily, sinking down onto a nearby chair and burying her face in her hands. 'I'm sorry to have been so hopeless...so feeble. I just couldn't seem to cope, somehow.'

'Well, I'm not surprised!' the other girl exclaimed, viewing Laura's hunched and trembling figure with some concern. 'Are you feeling OK?'

'Yes, I'll be all right in a minute,' she mumbled. 'Besides, I haven't yet paid the removal men—although how I'll ever be able to face them again I've no idea.'

'Leave it to me,' Susie said firmly. 'In the meantime, it's obvious that we both need a strong drink. So just relax and I'll be back in a moment.

'Here we are,' the blonde girl said a few minutes later, pressing a glass of tawny amber liquid into Laura's hands. 'I've settled up with the movers—I reckon we can finish the job ourselves—and I borrowed a bottle of brandy from the office next door. It seems to be a business travel firm, run by a couple of rather dishy men,' she added with a grin. 'Maybe I'll chat them up and see if I can't get hold of some free air tickets.'

'You're incorrigible!' Laura smiled weakly at the other girl.

'Well, at least I've got better things to do than moon over my ex-boss!' Susie informed her bluntly. 'Why on earth didn't you tell me that you're madly in love with Jack Wilder?'

'Are you crazy?' Laura gave a shrill, high-pitched shriek of laughter which even to her own ears sounded remarkably unconvincing. 'In any case, I *did* give you fair warning that Jack and I can't stand each other,' she protested. 'So why on earth you should think...? I mean, how could I *possibly* be in love with that...that thoroughly aggressive, nasty and amazingly arrogant man who's obviously nothing but a total louse?'

'How, indeed?' the other girl murmured drily.

'If you want to know the truth I really, *really* hate the rotten swine!' Laura continued, in the hope that by saying it loudly and often she could somehow persuade herself, and the rest of the world, that she spoke nothing but the truth.

'OK,' Susie sighed, beginning to realise that her new job was going to entail some unexpected and quite unforeseen complications. 'I'll try and pretend that I *didn't* see an amazingly hot, torrid embrace taking place in front of my very own eyes only half an hour ago! In fact, now I come to think about it, maybe I ought to go out and buy myself a new pair of dark glasses?'

'You do that!' Laura snapped, and immediately felt contrite. 'I'm sorry,' she whispered, hanging her head in shame. 'It's just...well, it's just been one hell of a day, and...'

'It's all right. There's no need to cry,' Susie murmured, putting a consoling arm about the slim shoulders of the girl sitting slumped in the chair, weak tears now trickling down her pale cheeks. 'You certainly aren't the first—nor likely to be the last—to make the mistake of falling for Mr Loverman's lethal charm.'

'I know...' Laura sniffed, fumbling in the pocket of her jeans for a handkerchief. 'That's why I was always so careful not to let Jack, or anyone else, guess how I felt about him. And then...then we w-went to T-Tahiti...' she sobbed.

'Come on—you'd better tell me all about it. If only so that we can try and avoid a repetition of what happened today. I honestly don't think my nerves can face too many rows like the one this morning,' Susie added with a slight laugh, before handing her a large box of tissues.

'Thanks for being so kind,' Laura muttered. 'I can't think what's come over me lately. I've never been the sort of person to dissolve into silly tears like this.'

'Love makes us do the strangest things,' the other girl agreed sagely. 'Now, dry your eyes and spill the beans. I promise that you'll feel a lot better after getting some of those problems off your chest.'

'Well...' Laura hesitated for a moment, and then, with a heavy sigh, she proceeded to relate what had happened between her and Jack in the hot, steamy atmosphere of the South Pacific. 'And then, when he suddenly gave me the sack, I...I just went to pieces,' she said and explained how, following her unfair and unreasonable dismissal, Jack had given the plum New York position in his new branch office to a totally incompetent colleague.

'To my mind it was a clear case of nepotism—Jack even admitted as much—and his offer of that awful job with Bill Chapman's voice-over firm was just about the *last* straw. Especially when Jack seemed to think that we were going to continue our affair just as if nothing had happened,' she added, blowing her nose and making a determined effort to pull herself together.

'He looked a bit shaken when I threatened to sue him for unreasonable dismissal. But, after giving the matter some thought, I couldn't see the point in making an already bad situation any worse.'

'You're right,' Susie agreed. 'I've read in the newspapers about some women in the City who've taken their employers to court and won their cases—only to find that no other firm will give them a job. It's totally unfair, of course, but there's nothing much they can do.'

Laura nodded and gave another heavy sigh. 'So I'm afraid that I said a lot of horrid things—although he did too, come to that!—and then kicked him out of my apartment, before ringing Donald and agreeing to start up this agency.'

'Do you think...?' The other girl hesitated for a moment. 'I mean, does Jack know that Donald is backing you?'

'I don't know.' Laura shrugged. 'I imagine that he's bound to find out sooner or later. Which will be yet *another* crime he'll lay at my door, if all those old stories about Donald and Melissa Grant are true.'

'Wow—the plot thickens!' Susie murmured. 'Well, if it's any consolation, I've *never* seen Jack so cut up, or watched him lose his temper in such a totally spectacular fashion. You must have really got under his skin!'

Laura blew her nose fiercely once more, realising that Susie had been quite right. She really did feel a whole lot better for being able to share her problems with the blonde girl.

'Well, I'm sorry to say that my behaviour has been almost as bad as Jack's,' she admitted sadly. 'I never used to like quarrelling or having noisy rows, like some people seem to do. But now he and I can't seem to be in the same room without being at each other's throats. And I'm very much afraid that he really *will* do his best to wreck this firm and put us out of business.

'Which is only fair—since I now have *every* intention of enticing away and stealing some of his best and most lucrative clients,' she added, with a snort of grim, tearful laughter. 'So I'll quite understand if you feel that you'd rather work for someone else.'

However, she was surprised by Susie's swift reaction.

'No way!' the other girl laughed. 'It may be a bumpy ride, but I wouldn't miss the forthcoming drama—not for all the tea in China! Besides, being Jack's personal assistant wasn't *exactly* a piece of cake,' she added. 'As you know, he expects his employees to work every bit as hard as he does—which meant it was all go from the moment I arrived in the morning until I flopped exhausted into bed at night.

'And, while I'm not afraid of hard work, or of putting in long hours whenever there's a problem to deal with, I'd have welcomed a word of thanks now and then. I was grateful for the annual bonus, of course, but we all need to feel appreciated, to know that we're a valued member of the firm, however lowly our status might be.'

'I'm sure Jack didn't mean to appear ungrateful,' Laura murmured, amazed to find herself coming to the awful man's defence.

'No, I don't suppose he did,' Susie agreed with a sigh. 'And neither did he really mean to take it out on me when things weren't going well. But that's men for you, isn't it?' She shrugged. 'Surely you must have noticed that a woman's place always seems to be in the wrong?'

'Tell me about it!' Laura grinned.

'Anyway... what I'm trying to say is that, while it was never boring working for Jack, he certainly doesn't command my undying loyalty,' Susie said firmly. 'Quite honestly, I think you ought to just concentrate on running *your* business and leave Jack to run his.'

Taking heart from Susie's words, and resolving to make sure that her new assistant always received due recognition and praise for a job well done, Laura was determined to heed her good advice.

Unfortunately, she'd already taken one or two decisions which, she now realised, had been extraordinarily foolish and likely to have dire consequences for her new business. So, if she now faced a 'bumpy ride', as Susie had predicted, she had no one to blame but herself.

Why, oh, *why* had she allowed her rage and fury with Jack to overtake her normal good sense? Because when he discovered what she had done he was almost certainly going to go completely *ballistic*!

CHAPTER FIVE

'DID you have a good weekend?' Laura called out as she passed Susie's office on the way towards her own. It was a lovely bright, sunny morning and she was feeling really excited at the prospect of this, their first morning as a fully registered theatrical agency.

'As it turned out, I *did* have rather a good time,' Susie said, following her into the now clean, tidy and efficient-looking office. 'Donald Hunt asked me out to dinner on Saturday night.'

Removing her smart emerald-green linen jacket, Laura smiled over at the small blonde girl leaning against the open doorway. 'Well, I can't say that I'm *entirely* surprised to hear that piece of news! I thought he'd taken quite a shine to you, right from the time of our first meeting.'

'Yes, well . . . he's a nice guy and we spent an amusing evening together.'

'Is Donald married?' Laura asked casually as she sat down, quickly scanning the papers on the desk in front of her.

She was very fond of her new assistant, their friendship having deepened over the past few weeks, when they'd spent so much time together. Which was why she was hoping that the other girl, still obviously bearing scars from the breakdown of her first marriage, wouldn't become embroiled in a messy affair with a married man.

Besides which they needed another broken heart in this office like fish need bicycles!

'No, as it happens, he isn't married,' Susie murmured airily, grinning as she caught the amused gleam in Laura's green eyes. 'I didn't like to ask too many leading questions, and it seemed a bit early in our friendship to bring up the subject of his affair with Jack's wife, Melissa. However, while there appear to have been one or two long-standing relationships in the past, it now seems that Donald is as free as a bird.'

'I'm glad to hear it.'

'Yes—so was I!' Susie laughed, before going back into her own office. Returning a few minutes later, she placed the opened post on Laura's desk, together with a typed list of the messages which had been left on their answering machine over the weekend.

'Oh, by the way—just before you arrived, we had some parcels delivered. It looks as if our office stationery has arrived at last.'

'That's great!' Laura said, lifting her phone as she prepared to return some of the calls. 'Can I leave you to sort it out?' she added quickly. 'Because I think I'm just about to take on another client.'

'No problem,' the other girl told her quickly, disappearing back into her own office and leaving Laura to chat up the young actor on whom she'd had her eye for some time.

Twenty minutes later, she leaned back in her chair, regarding the notes in front of her with satisfaction. The word had soon got out, of course. The acting profession seemed to operate on an extraordinarily efficient grapevine, with news of forthcoming productions and job opportunities whizzing through their ranks with the speed of light. So the information that Laura Parker had decided to start up her own theatrical agency, and was busy looking for young, bright and talented actors, had resulted in a host of applications.

Unfortunately, however talented they might be, there were very few youngsters whom she could afford to take on to her books at the moment. It would only be when she was well established, with one or two clients capable of earning a great deal of money, that she could afford to use the fees gained by those actors to subsidise and encourage those just starting out on their careers.

Luckily, she'd built up a good relationship in the past with various casting directors—especially ones dealing with long-running TV programmes. And, provided she was careful not to put forward any clients who were simply not up to the job, she could look forward to having some of her new actors start work almost immediately.

But what she *really* needed at the moment—if only to prove to Jack Wilder that she was perfectly capable of running a successful business—was at least one well-known star; an actor of either sex who commanded both high fees and universal respect. She had, of course, an exciting idea at the back of her mind. But pulling it off wasn't going to be easy.

'I've unpacked all the stationery,' Susie said, coming into the room. 'I think it looks great, and these visiting cards are really very smart indeed,' she added, placing a small cardboard box down on Laura's desk. 'The only thing is...'

'Mmm?'

'Well...' Susie hesitated for a moment, frowning as she gazed down at the sheet of new paper in her hand.

'I'm not sure... Don't get me wrong!' she added hastily. 'Because I reckon that Worldwide Artists Management is a really brilliant name for your new theatrical agency. Apart from anything else, it has a terrifically solid and stylish ring to it. But it's just occurred to me that the initials are remarkably similar to those of our old firm.'

'Oh, really...?' Laura murmured, continuing to study the notes on the pad in front of her.

Susie went on looking at the piece of paper with a puzzled expression on her face, before raising her eyes to stare in speculation at the faint flush on Laura's cheeks.

'Oh, no! I simply don't *believe* it!' the blonde girl gasped as the awful truth slowly began to dawn on her. 'You didn't...? You can't have...?'

'I can't have—what?' Laura muttered, still seemingly intent on studying the papers before her.

'You did it quite deliberately, didn't you?' Susie breathed. 'Oh, my God—Jack Wilder will go absolutely *berserk*!'

As her assistant's horrified voice seemed to echo around the large office, Laura put down her pen and leaned back in her chair.

'I can't think why you're making such a fuss. There is absolutely *no* similarity between Worldwide Artists Management and Wilder, Hunt and Martin. In fact, the names of the two businesses couldn't be more different,' she added with a careless shrug of her shoulder, her eyes not quite meeting Susie's troubled gaze.

'The names may be completely dissimilar but the *initials* are virtually the same,' Susie pointed out grimly. 'And if you think Jack *isn't* going to notice that small but important detail you must need your head examined!'

'Rubbish! Why should it matter to him one way or another?'

'Do me a favour!' The other girl gave a heavy sigh, grimacing as she raised her eyes to the ceiling as if praying for divine guidance.

'You and I both know that, with such similar initials, many of Jack's clients are likely to be confused when they study the notice-board down in the foyer,' Susie continued impatiently. 'In fact, faced with two firms— WAM and WHAM—they'll probably call in to *this* office first, by mistake—right? Not to mention all the ghastly muddles and fuss over phone calls and postal delivery.'

Laura shrugged. 'I really think that you're taking all this far too seriously, and—'

'Come off it!' Susie gave a hollow laugh, shaking her head at the sheer folly being perpetrated by her new employer. 'There's no point in bothering to pretend that it's a mistake. Because I know you, Laura, and it's *just* the sort of thing you'd do if you wanted to make Jack's life particularly tiresome and difficult!'

'Yes, well...' Laura sighed heavily, realising that there was no point in continuing to deny that it had been a deliberate action on her part. 'I'm ashamed to say that you're quite right.'

'But you must have known that it was a really crazy thing to do?'

'Yes, I suppose so,' Laura agreed, with an unhappy shrug of her slim shoulders. 'But, to tell the truth, I think I must have been temporarily out of my head when I went down to Companies House to register the name of the new business. All I could think about was trying to get even with Jack.' She gave another heavy sigh before lapsing into an unhappy silence.

'Well, it's obviously too late to do anything about it now,' Susie told her with a wry shake of her blonde head. 'So I guess we'll just have to ride out the storm. Which, if I'm not mistaken, is likely to break over our heads any minute!'

However, when a week had passed without producing the expected thunder and lightning from Jack Wilder, Laura gradually relaxed. In fact, she was far too busy to spend any time wondering about Jack's reaction to the name of her new firm, because Worldwide Artists Management was having great success in attracting both clients and interesting jobs.

And, as the working week drew to a close, that success was crowned by the news that one of her particularly gifted young actresses had landed a plum role in a long-running and very successful TV comedy, thus gaining both a substantial salary for the actress and considerable kudos for Laura's new company.

She wasn't prepared, therefore, for the harsh, grating voice on her phone when she returned to her office the following Monday.

'I want you upstairs in my office within the next five minutes—*or else*!'

There was no need for the caller to identify himself. Laura immediately recognised Jack's deep voice.

'Or else—what?' she retorted, playing for time as she tried to think how she was going to deal with the situation.

'Or else I'll be coming down—*to tear you personally limb from limb*!' he hissed savagely, before loudly banging down his phone.

Refusing to dance to the damned man's tune, Laura spent the next seven minutes applying fresh make-up and brushing her hair. If she was about to be shot down in flames, then at least she was going down with all colours flying! However, after a quick glance down at her wrist-watch, she realised that it would be foolish to push her luck too far.

'If I'm not back in half an hour, you'd better send in the troops,' she told Susie with a nervous laugh, after having briefly put the other girl in the picture.

Grateful for her assistant's restraint in not saying 'I told you so', Laura left her office, hurrying down the passage towards the bank of lifts. Impatiently tapping her foot and jabbing irritably at the buttons, she wasted two precious minutes before remembering that three out of four lifts were being serviced that morning. So, quickly deciding that it definitely wasn't a good idea to add any more fuel to the flames of Jack's anger, she rapidly made her way to the stairs leading up to the next floor.

Walking as swiftly as she could along the thickly carpeted corridor leading to her old offices, she couldn't help feeling a certain sense of *déjà vu*. There had rarely been an occasion, during the years in which she had worked for Jack, when she hadn't approached this door with feelings of pleasure and anticipation. Unfortunately, however much she was determined to hide the fact, her feelings today were mainly composed of nervous apprehension and dread.

Even leaving aside her forthcoming confrontation with Jack himself—and she certainly wasn't looking forward to that encounter!—Laura knew that it might prove awkward meeting some of her old colleagues. Following her noisy, extremely acrimonious departure from the office all those weeks ago, and the fact that she'd now set up in direct opposition to her old firm, it was more than likely that she'd be given the cold shoulder.

As she neared the main door leading to Jack's agency Laura took a deep breath, desperately trying to control the rising panic and tension sweeping through her body. Stay cool—and for heaven's sake calm down! she told herself sternly, pausing for a moment to straighten her short-sleeved navy blue jacket over its matching, slim-fitting dress.

Thank goodness that she'd laid down a policy for both herself and Susie of always being fashionably and smartly dressed in the office. While this had been originally decided upon as a way of demonstrating to clients that they were dealing with an efficient, up-market firm, she did now have the satisfaction of knowing that, if nothing else, she was looking elegant and businesslike.

Taking a deep breath and assuming a confident smile that was sharply at variance with the butterflies causing mayhem in her stomach, Laura sailed into her old office. And while there were, of course, one or two of her old colleagues who pretended that they'd never seen her before—with Betty, Jack's secretary, giving her a particularly sour glance of pure hostility through her thick pebble glasses—it was comforting to receive a beaming smile from the young receptionist.

'It's great to see you again, Laura,' she said, giving her an enthusiastic hug, before leading her towards the oak door guarding Jack's office.

'You took your time!' he barked, scowling from behind his desk at Laura's slim, self-assured figure as she walked confidently over the carpet towards him.

Laura gave a shrug of her shoulders. 'They still seem to be having trouble with the lifts in this building,' she explained quietly, swiftly deciding that a soft, concili-atory approach would be best in dealing with the rigidly angry figure glaring at her from the other side of the room.

'However, I'm sorry if I'm late,' she added with a slight, placatory smile, sitting down on a black leather chair in front of his desk.

'I don't suppose I have to tell you exactly *why* you're here?' Jack drawled, his voice heavy with sarcasm.

'Well, yes, actually you do,' she murmured, before turning her gaze on the silent figure of a woman standing in the window. 'I don't think I've met...?'

'This is Felicity Green,' he said brusquely, waving a hand in the direction of the other girl. 'She's just joined the firm—to fill your old position.'

'I'm sure that you'll enjoy your time here. It's a great agency,' Laura said brightly, despite viewing the statu-esque blonde—and her curvaceous figure—with some considerable dismay.

No one had any *right* to have a figure like that—or to look quite so beautiful, Laura told herself grimly as the other girl murmured a polite response. And, what was more, Felicity was also bound to be as bright as blazes, because Jack—other than his calculated risk with dopey Henry—would never employ anyone stupid. Unless, of course, he'd suddenly decided to change the policy of no hanky-panky in his office? Because how anyone—let alone Jack—could manage to keep his hands off this particular girl she had no idea.

'Felicity trained at Scott Marshall before going to work for ICM,' Jack drawled, clearly intending to let Laura know that, despite the other girl's amazing chest measurement, she was no dumb bunny. 'She has a first-class degree from Oxford, and she also speaks three languages,' he added enthusiastically, obviously hoping to rub salt in the wound.

'Oh, really? That's great,' Laura murmured, casually leaning back in her chair and crossing one leg over her knee, as if she hadn't a care in the world. 'Now, what exactly did you want to see me about?'

'You know damn well why you're here!' he told her roughly. 'And I'm not prepared to put up with any more nonsense. How you had the brass cheek to pick that name for your new firm I really don't know, but—'

'Excuse me,' she interjected quickly. 'Are we talking about my new business?'

'We most certainly are!'

'Well, I'm sorry, Jack, but you seem to have forgotten that I'm no longer your employee,' she pointed out. 'And, while I'd like to be helpful, I'm really not prepared to discuss my private business affairs in front of junior members of your staff,' she added, turning to give the girl standing by the window a brief, apologetic smile.

'You're in no position to dictate terms to me,' he retorted grimly.

'Oh, really...?' she murmured coolly, lowering her gaze to inspect the pale pink polish on her perfectly manicured nails.

Determinedly ignoring both Felicity's muttered protest and Jack's promise of dire retribution if she didn't *immediately* answer his question, Laura continued the inspection of her nails, until the sound of fury filling the office gradually gave way to a heavy silence.

'All right,' Jack said at last, impatiently waving the other girl from the room. 'But I'm damned well going to get the truth out of you—come hell or high water!'

Laura waited until the door had closed behind the se-
ductive, hourglass figure of Felicity before raising her
eyes to face him.

'That's better,' she smiled. 'Now perhaps we can have
a civilised discussion?'

He gave a muffled snort of sardonic laughter. 'I very
much doubt it!' he told her wryly, some of the anger
clearly draining from his body as he leaned back in his
chair. 'In fact, Laura, while I'm prepared to admire your
sheer brazen effrontery, I'm afraid that "civilised" is
definitely *not* the word that immediately springs to mind
when describing our relationship!'

'Oh, dear. I'm sorry to hear that.'

'OK—you can cut out this nauseous, sickly sweet Mary
Poppins attitude—which I assume you've adopted solely
to annoy me? Because, you'll be glad to hear, it's suc-
ceeding admirably!' he ground out angrily, leaning
forward on his desk once more. 'I want to know *exactly*
what you thought you were doing in choosing a name
for your new firm which is, to all intents and purposes,
exactly the same as my agency's.'

Laura gave a weak laugh. 'Really, Jack, you must
know that you're talking moonshine! Wherever did you
get the idea that...?'

'When Betty saw your firm's name on the list of
companies in the foyer downstairs, she immediately
pointed the problem out to me.'

'Oh, right! So *Betty* has decided she doesn't like the
name of my firm, has she?'

'It's not just Betty,' he retorted curtly. 'I've been very
busy lately, but as soon as she pointed out the problem
I saw that she was quite right. The initials of our two
businesses are practically the same. And I'm telling you,

here and now,' he added forcibly, banging his fist down hard on the desk, 'that I am *not* prepared to put up with any of this nonsense. If you don't change the name of your new agency right away, I'll take steps to force you to do so.'

Laura stared at him silently for a moment. 'I don't know what to say,' she said at last, with a helpless shrug of her slim shoulders. 'I can hardly believe that you're making *all* this fuss over something which seems to have arisen solely from Betty's overheated imagination.

'OK, OK...' she continued quickly as his dark brows drew menacingly together in a deep frown. 'Yes, I can see, if you're *really* looking for trouble, that you might possibly claim that the two businesses have similar initials. But it beats me why you should think it was a deliberate action on my part. Why on earth would I do such a thing?'

'To cause me the maximum amount of annoyance— that's why!' he retorted promptly through clenched teeth. 'I know you, Laura, and it's *just* the sort of evil-minded trick you'd play. Especially if you thought it would cause me any trouble or grief.'

Shaken by the fact that Susie and Jack had both used almost the same words, and come to the very same quick conclusion about her character, Laura found herself wondering if she really *was* turning out to be such a thoroughly nasty person, after all. But, however depressing a prospect it might be, there wasn't anything she could do about it at the moment. Not when she had to concentrate on trying to persuade Jack that she was as pure as the driven snow. Although quite how she was going to pull it off she had no idea. Maybe assuming a thoroughly hurt, wounded attitude might work...?

'Well, I'm sorry, Jack, but I'm *really* upset by these completely *wild* accusations,' she protested with a sniff, as if she might burst into tears at any moment. 'If you hadn't thrown me out of this firm and . . . and ruined my life...I'd never have been forced to try to earn my living as best I could. It's not *my* fault that I'm now struggling to make ends meet, and—'

'Put a sock in it, Laura!' he interjected grimly. 'Believe me, I've had *far* better actresses than you in here trying exactly the same sort of trick. And I can tell you that it didn't work for them, either!' he added with a harsh bark of sardonic laughter. 'So you can forget those false tears—not to mention the heart-wrenching, ''pathetic little me'' speech. Because I'm *still* waiting to hear what you're going to do about changing the name of your new agency.'

How could I have thought that this awful man was the *slightest* bit attractive—let alone fallen in love with him? she asked herself incredulously, scowling across the desk at her old employer, who was obviously a deeply unpleasant human being.

'Well, dream on, Jack! Because, while it may come as a bit of a shock to you, I do have rather *more* important things on my mind at the moment,' she told him scathingly. 'So, if you want to run around squawking like a chicken without its head, then that's up to you. But as far as I'm concerned,' she added, rising to her feet, 'I've wasted quite enough time listening to this nonsense.'

'I'm not letting this matter rest,' he warned her grimly. 'I'll be taking it up with Companies House first thing in the morning.'

'Fine. Go right ahead. Sue me in the High Court if you want to. Why should I care?' she told him, waving a hand idly in the air. 'Especially since my new business could do with the publicity!' she added with a laugh, turning to walk towards the door.

She had only taken one or two steps before she heard him give an exasperated heavy sigh. 'Come and sit down, Laura,' he commanded grimly. 'I think it's about time we sorted out a few ground rules and buried the hatchet—don't you?'

Almost sagging with relief, she pretended to hesitate for a moment, before slowly retracing her steps. Quite undeservedly, as it turned out, it was beginning to look as though she'd managed to wriggle off the hook. And if Jack—who really *did* have good reason to be thoroughly fed up and furious with her—was prepared to be reasonable, then it was about time she pulled herself together. Quickly resolving not to be so foolish and stupid in future, she gratefully accepted the olive branch he was now holding out to her.

'OK—I'm willing to bury the hatchet if you are. And besides,' she admitted with a slight shrug, 'I haven't got a large office staff at my disposal. Since I'm virtually running a one-man band, I really can't afford to spend time quarrelling with you.'

'I'm glad you've decided to be sensible at last,' he said, continuing to regard her with a stern, beady eye. 'However, I don't trust you one inch, Laura—you're as artful as a cageful of monkeys. So I'm going to insist on one, firm condition for not having the pleasure of wringing your damned neck!'

'And that is?'

'You're going to have lunch with me next week. I don't care *what* other arrangements you may have,' he told her as she opened her mouth to protest. 'I'll expect you to be at The Ivy promptly at one o'clock on Friday. And woe betide you if you're late!' he added, a warning rasp in his deep voice.

Laura eyed him warily. What in the hell was Jack up to now? She been around long enough to know that both The Ivy and Le Caprice—the favourite restaurants of actors and film stars, as well as top agents, producers and directors—would normally be way out of her league, and were generally booked solid for many weeks ahead.

'Well—have we got a deal?' he demanded curtly.

She shrugged. 'Yes, I suppose so. But I can't think why—'

'It seems as if the whole theatrical industry has been enjoying the spectacle of you and me at one another's throats,' he told her grimly. 'And, while I don't know about your business, it's certainly not doing *my* firm any good,' he added, his lips tight with annoyance.

'However, kindly *don't* make the mistake of imagining that I have any ulterior motive,' he continued in a hard, cold voice. 'Any feelings which I might once have had for you are now well and truly dead. So we will have a highly visible lunch, which should effectively scotch any rumours about the in-fighting between your office and mine. And then, with any luck, I'll *never* have to set eyes on you again.'

And that was just about it, as she subsequently told Susie, after returning, thoroughly chastened, to her own office.

'I've obviously been a complete idiot. So I've got no one to blame but myself,' she admitted with a gloomy sigh.

'Never mind.' Susie shrugged. 'It's over now, and I don't suppose that you're going to make that sort of mistake again in a hurry. Oh, by the way,' she added, 'I hear, on the grapevine, that Jack has now appointed a girl to take over your old job. Did you see her?'

Laura nodded, sinking down into the chair behind her desk and wondering why, when she'd just had such a lucky escape from Jack's fully justified wrath, she should be feeling so unhappy and depressed. Maybe it had something to do with the tension headache, which had started to make itself felt halfway through her recent, fraught interview and was now beginning to throb in earnest.

'So, what's she like?' Susie asked impatiently, obviously dying to hear the latest gossip concerning their old firm.

Laura shrugged and gave a heavy sigh, before resting her aching head on the back of her chair. 'Well...it seems that her name is Felicity Green. Not only is she multilingual and obviously very clever, she also has a truly *amazing* figure. On top of which, I imagine she's likely to cause total havoc amongst the red-blooded male population in this building—because there's no doubt that she's one of the most beautiful girls I've ever seen.'

'*Oh, dear!*' Susie muttered, fervently wishing that she'd kept her mouth shut.

'Yes...those two words just about sum up my own reaction,' Laura admitted with another heavy sigh as she continued to stare blankly up at the ceiling. 'Jack seemed highly delighted with his new assistant, of course. What's more, I was left with the distinct impression that, while Felicity may be able to speak three or four languages, she isn't likely to say "no" in any one of them!'

Laura closed the book, smiling and shaking her head as the two small boys tried to persuade her to read them one more story.

'It's no good trying to twist my arm.' She grinned at her nephews. 'Because your mother won't be at all pleased if I'm late for supper.'

'She's quite right—I won't!' her sister agreed, putting her head around the door and sternly telling her two young sons that it was time they went off to sleep.

Leaving Amy to kiss her children goodnight, Laura walked slowly down the stairs and into the large sitting room, before sinking down into a wide comfortable chair with a deep sigh of relief.

'You look completely exhausted.' Her brother-in-law gazed at her with concern as he handed her a drink. 'It's about time you had a holiday.'

'Oh, come on, Tom—you must be joking!' Laura gave a snort of wry laughter as she leaned wearily back against the cushions, gratefully sipping her stiff gin and tonic. 'A holiday is one of those luxuries I can't afford now I'm running my own business. Not because of any serious financial problems,' she added hurriedly, just in case he might think she was pleading poverty. 'But I really daren't leave the office for too long at the moment. Not when the next phone call might lead to an important deal for one of my clients.'

'While I realise that you were more or less forced to start up your own theatrical agency, it does seem to be taking a lot out of you.' Her brother-in-law frowned. 'I hope you feel that it's worth it?'

'There speaks the academic!' Laura teased. 'But quite honestly, Tom, I've got to do *something* with my life—and I don't know much about anything other than looking after and guiding the careers of those in the theatrical profession.' She shrugged. 'Although I'm not going to pretend that it's particularly valuable work, like medicine or the law, there's no doubt that films, TV and the theatre do help to brighten people's lives. However, you're quite right. It *is* hard work, and so I've just got to hope that it's going to be worth it in the end, haven't I?'

It wasn't until they were halfway through a delicious supper that Amy's husband once more raised the subject of her new business, and whether she could really make a success of what seemed to him to be a very perilous profession.

'Well, I honestly don't know if I am going to succeed.' Laura gave a helpless shrug. 'I've had to work flat out from day one, of course, simply because there are so many gifted people chasing so few jobs. And it isn't just a case of making a few phone calls and happily pocketing a percentage of the actor's fee,' she explained. 'To be really successful in this business, I'm going to need at least one seriously big star on my books.'

'But why should one person, however famous, make the difference between success and failure?' Amy demanded, gazing at her with a puzzled frown.

'Well, it may sound mad, but success in my business doesn't necessarily reflect the financial standing of a firm. I suppose it's all a matter of confidence,' Laura added, brushing a tired hand through her auburn hair. 'For instance, I'm involved in *very* secret negotiations with a well-known film star at the moment. So *if* I can get him to sign a contract with my firm, *and* find him a really juicy part in a play or film, then many of his colleagues are going to begin thinking that maybe I can do exactly the same thing for them.'

'Aha!' Amy laughed. 'So what you're saying is: the better actors you can get on your books, the more exciting jobs you can attract from producers and directors—right?'

'Got it in one!' Laura grinned, before adding with a weary shrug, 'But while it sounds easy enough in theory it's actually *very* difficult to achieve in practice.'

'Oh, I'm quite sure you won't have any trouble,' Amy told her firmly, which left Laura wishing she were half as confident as her sister. Not that she wasn't grateful for such family support, but it didn't go very far in the hard, tough world of theatrical management.

Unfortunately, Amy—normally such a down-to-earth and level-headed woman—suddenly seemed to have become fascinated by the news and gossip about Laura's profession, and was demanding to know the name of the film star with whom her sister was having secret negotiations.

'There's no way I'm going to tell you—I haven't even broken the news to Susie, for heaven's sake,' Laura protested. But whether she was feeling particularly brain-dead that evening, or whether it was because her elder sister had always managed to extract the truth from her, Laura eventually gave in and revealed that she'd been talking to Craig Jordan.

'But I thought you didn't like him?'

'You're quite right—I don't,' Laura agreed. 'But it's strictly a business deal between Craig and myself. He's a big name, and I want him in *my* agency. Besides, there's a good chance that I can get him a really great part in a new film.'

'But...but I thought that his career was being managed by Jack Wilder?' Her sister frowned in confusion.

'Well, yes... at the moment he *does* have a contract with Jack,' Laura admitted, shifting uneasily in her chair as she realised—from the wide grin on her brother-in-law's face—that, unlike his wife, Tom had a very good idea of what she was planning.

'You're so sharp you'll cut yourself one of these days!' she told him with a grim smile, before turning back to Amy. 'Since I used to work in Jack's office, I happen to know that Craig's contract is due for renewal in a month's time.'

'Oh, *Laura*!' her sister exclaimed, gazing at the younger girl with concern. 'Surely Jack will be very angry if Craig decides to sign up with you?'

'Well, yes—he'll probably be absolutely furious. But that's his bad luck!' she added defiantly, her cheeks flushing as her sister gave a heavy sigh and shook her head in disapproval. 'After all, as Jack himself told me only a few weeks ago, it's a rat race, and you can't afford to be too squeamish in our business.'

'But why do you always seem *so* determined to look for trouble?' Amy exclaimed anxiously. 'Why do something which you *know* is going to lead to an almighty row with Jack Wilder?'

However, before Laura could reply, her brother-in-law stepped firmly into the temporary breach between the two sisters, strongly urging his wife not to get involved in the ongoing conflict between Laura and her old boss.

'This is obviously a highly volatile relationship between two very strong personalities,' Tom added, his lips twitching with wry amusement. 'So I suggest that we'd do well to leave them to sort out their own problems—in their own way!'

'OK,' Amy muttered, quickly realising that her husband was, as usual, quite right. And, since she hated quarrelling with her younger sister, she decided to do her best to ignore the problems which were obviously looming on the horizon for Laura.

'So tell me about this film you have in mind for Craig,' Amy said, pouring them all another cup of coffee. 'Will it be made in Hollywood?'

'No, I'm afraid not. And, while it's a terrific role for Craig, I must say that it's not exactly top box-office material,' Laura explained, grateful to have avoided a row with her sister, whom she loved dearly. 'On top of which, the production has been plagued by a series of disastrous accidents. In fact, every time shooting is about to start, one or other of the leading actors seems to fall by the wayside.'

'What ever do you mean?'

Laura grinned. 'I'm sorry. I should have said that the film is based on Shakespeare's play *Macbeth*. For some reason, most of the acting profession think that the play is dead unlucky. So much so that it's supposed to be tempting fate to even say the name of the play out loud. And I must admit,' she added reflectively, 'they may have a point. Because the latest victim to fall foul of the "curse"—the film star due to play the part of Macbeth himself—has just been involved in a fairly horrendous car smash.'

'Good heavens!' Amy breathed.

'I feel really sorry for the producer, whom I've known since we were both at university together. However, since he's obviously anxious to start filming, before the financiers get cold feet and withdraw funding, there's a very good chance I can get Craig the part.'

'But what if he has an accident too?'

Laura laughed and shook her head. 'No chance! Craig may well be a fairly poisonous individual, but I suspect he bears a charmed life. In fact, on the principle that the good die young, Craig Jordan will undoubtedly still be around to collect a telegram from the Queen on his hundredth birthday!'

Maybe she'd been just a *little* hard on Craig, Laura told herself as she returned home later that evening. But not much. In fact, if she'd had the opportunity to get hold of another actor, she certainly would have done so. Because, despite what Tom and Amy might think, she definitely wasn't looking for trouble with Jack Wilder— who'd almost certainly be absolutely *livid* to lose such a well-known, prestigious client.

CHAPTER SIX

FORCING her way through the paparazzi waiting patiently outside the restaurant in the hopes of catching a sneaky, off-duty photo of one of the many celebrities within, Laura paused on the threshold of The Ivy, looking about her with some confusion.

Goodness, it was crowded! Quickly scanning the tables in the large, wood-panelled room, she only took a few seconds to recognise many famous faces normally to be seen on the wide cinema screen or on large billboards outside the London theatres.

'Absolutely bang on time—well done!' Jack grinned, rising to his feet as she was conducted to his table. 'I should have remembered that you were always a good timekeeper.'

'Well, it's nice to know that I did *something* right,' she muttered as a waiter drew out a chair for her to sit down, before placing a large linen napkin on her lap.

It was stupid of her, of course, but she'd been really dreading this lunch date. It had also taken her simply ages to decide what to wear, since undoubtedly many of the theatrical in-crowd would be dressed up to the nines. But now, as she glanced casually around the restaurant, Laura was relieved to note that her pale pink collarless jacket over a slim-fitting black linen dress, sheer black stockings and high-heeled black patent leather shoes had been the right choice after all.

However, leaving aside her apprehension about her clothes, it had been the forthcoming meeting with Jack himself which had caused her so much nervous stress and apprehension. She had, of course, repeatedly told herself that it was downright foolish—not to say totally pathetic!—to be getting into such a state about a mere lunch date. But, while Jack had made it crystal-clear that he was no longer interested in her, in any shape or form, she hadn't been nearly so successful at removing his dark presence from both her heart and mind.

How *did* one manage to crush and exterminate all feelings of love and tenderness? Because she, for one, would have been happy to know the answer. Over the past four days, Laura had done everything she could to try and eradicate the deep feelings which, she realised only too well, had now no hope of being reciprocated. And while she had been partly successful during the day—so busy with her new business that she'd had no opportunity to think about anything other than the matter in hand—the nights were quite a different matter.

Goodness knows, she'd tried just about every trick in the book in the desperate search for a good night's sleep. But all to no avail. If and when she did manage to drop off, she was plagued by vivid, harrowing dreams, all featuring Jack in a dramatic starring role. So many times she'd woken up drenched with sweat and trembling for the comfort of his arms—a comfort which she knew to be hopelessly beyond her reach.

'This is supposed to be a friendly working lunch—remember?' Jack's voice cut through her glum thoughts. 'We're not going to achieve anything if you continue to look as though you're just about to attend a funeral.'

Raising her eyes quickly to his face, she was momentarily confused and almost thrown off balance by the warmth of his broad smile. And then, quickly remembering exactly *why* she was here and the role she was expected to perform, Laura ruthlessly stifled the small flicker of hope that had flared so briefly in her wounded heart.

Taking a deep, unsteady breath, she flashed him a brilliant smile designed to convince any onlooker that she was having the time of her life.

'OK, Mr Loverman—how do you want to play this game?' she cooed sweetly through clenched teeth. 'Are we supposed to hold hands and gaze longingly into each other's eyes? Only make up your mind quickly, because the effort of keeping on smiling at you like this is already making me feel quite ill!'

To her surprise, Jack merely responded to her words with what she could have sworn was a snort of genuine laughter. Leaning back in his seat, his shoulders shaking with amusement, he was prevented from saying any more as the waiter came up to take their order.

When they were alone once more, Jack regarded her silently for a moment, before saying, 'I hadn't really thought how to "play" it. However, I see no reason why we can't just have a pleasant meal without coming to blows. Or is that too much to expect?' he added with a grin.

'Well, I won't make any promises. But I guess I'm willing to suspend hostilities if you are,' she agreed cautiously.

'Good. And now, having got the ground rules sorted out, I'm going to chance my arm by saying that you're looking absolutely stunning! I always think it's a pity that more...er...*auburn*-haired women don't wear that particular shade of pink,' he said with a smile. 'In fact, my dear Laura, I must say that you look almost good enough to eat!'

'Um...er...thank you,' she muttered nervously, completely taken aback by the unexpected words of appreciation. And especially from *this* man—who must know what he's talking about, since he's had more glamorous girlfriends than you've had hot dinners! Laura reminded herself, while at the same time trying to control the warm, happy glow spreading through her nervous figure. It would, after all, be *extremely* foolish of her to read anything significant into what had, after all, been nothing more than an idle compliment.

'I'd also like to congratulate you on the success of your new company,' Jack continued with an engaging smile. 'I'm willing to admit that I didn't think you had a cat in hell's chance of making a go of it. But you clearly have. So well done—and good luck in the future!'

Regarding him warily from beneath her eyelashes, her ears finely tuned to catch any note of irony of cynicism, Laura was forced to the conclusion that, however astonishing it might seem, Jack really did mean what he said. And while, of course, it could be *the* performance of a lifetime, she really had no option but to accept his congratulations—and the glass he was holding out to her in salutation—at face value.

Maybe it was the effect of the delicious food and wine, but with her ex-employer clearly setting out to be an entertaining companion she found it virtually impossible to maintain her original aggression. They did, after all, have so much in common—both in the careers of various clients, which she'd looked after when working in his office, and some of her newly acquired young actors, about whom Jack was proving to be very helpful.

'You'll need to keep a close eye on Brat Tyler,' he warned. 'The boy's enormously talented, of course. But I suspect that if Brat isn't his real name he's definitely earned it over the past two years! I hear that getting him to turn up on time at auditions can be a complete nightmare. And I know for a fact that he's driven at least two theatrical agencies completely up the wall,' Jack added with a rueful laugh. 'However, providing you keep a firm hand on the lad—*and* organise transport to take him to auditions!—he could turn out to be a real star.'

'Thanks for the advice.' She grinned companionably at him, suddenly wishing that it could always be like this. Maybe, if and when she ever managed to fall out of love with this devastatingly attractive man, it might be possible for them to become friends?

However, on one level at least there was no doubt that the lunch was proving to be a great success. Throughout the meal, people either waved to them across the room or came over to greet Jack as they passed to and from their tables. Since he always made a point of introducing Laura, and explaining that they were here to celebrate her new business venture, it was made clear that any stories of ill will and bitter animosity between them had absolutely no foundation at all.

'That was a very enjoyable lunch, in more ways than one,' Jack said as they finally left the restaurant. 'Thank you for helping to turn what could have been a difficult occasion into a considerable success.'

There was no mistaking the note of genuine appreciation in his voice, and Laura found herself feeling absurdly pleased and happy for the first time in many weeks. Which was perhaps why, as they walked back to the office down West Street and into Shaftesbury Avenue, his next remark came as a shattering bolt from the blue.

'By the way,' he murmured casually, taking her arm as they crossed the road, 'I heard an *extraordinary* piece of gossip the other day. Apparently, Craig Jordan is thinking of leaving my firm. In fact, rumour says that when his contract comes up for renewal at the end of this month he's proposing to join someone who's set up a brand-new theatrical agency. I don't suppose *you* know anything about it . . . ?'

'Me?' She stopped and turned to stare up at him, her eyes wide with shock and horror, before quickly forcing herself to give a shrill peal of laughter. 'Really, Jack! I know you like a good joke—but this is ridiculous! Surely you haven't forgotten that I simply can't *stand* Craig?'

'No, I haven't,' he agreed smoothly. 'But, since I also harbour feelings of intense dislike towards the wretched man, I really don't think that's very important—do you?'

'Well . . .'

'However,' Jack continued grimly, 'I can promise to be very, *very* angry if I find your delicate footprints anywhere *near* Craig Jordan!'

Speechless, desperately trying to think of something to say which didn't involve her becoming caught up in a tissue of lies, Laura was pathetically grateful to be saved by the sight of a tall, beautiful blonde girl waving to them as she left the office building some yards away.

'I think you've already met my new assistant,' he said, returning the girl's wave as she walked down the street towards them.

'Really . . . ?' she murmured, deliberately injecting a slightly puzzled note into her voice. 'Oh, yes—of course

I have,' she added, with a low gurgle of caustic laughter. 'How could I *possibly* have forgotten meeting dear Felicity—the thinking man's Easter bunny?'

'At least she's easy on the eye—and TV producers just *love* dealing with her. What did they used to call you, Laura?' he taunted savagely. 'Saddam Hussein in a miniskirt...?'

One of these fine days I'm *really* going to kill this bastard! Laura promised herself grimly, unable to believe that he could be so desperately unfair. Unfortunately, as Felicity was now only a few feet away, there was no opportunity to remind him that, simply *because* of her hard, tough bargaining skills, many of his clients were now earning a decent wage from some of the more tight-fisted TV companies.

Determinedly ignoring both the insult and the tightly clenched fingers painfully digging into her arm, she gave his new assistant a beaming smile.

'Hello, Felicity—how's it going?' she asked brightly. 'Is my old boss keeping your nose to the grindstone?'

'Yes...er...I suppose so...' the other girl murmured, her gaze shifting nervously between the hard, stormy expression on Jack's handsome face and the attractive red-headed girl, whose emerald-green eyes appeared to be glittering with overwhelming rage and fury.

'Well, if you have a job without aggravation, you don't have a job—right?' Laura gave a high-pitched laugh, before adroitly twisting free of the hand which had been so cruelly gripping her arm. 'I'm sorry I can't stop,' she added, giving them both a wide, beaming and entirely false smile. 'Unfortunately, I've *so* many important contracts to be signed...I really *must* dash!'

'How did the lunch go?' Susie called out as Laura returned to the office, hurrying swiftly past her assistant on her way into her own room and throwing herself down into the chair behind her desk. 'Was it really awful?' she continued sympathetically as her employer snatched up the phone, rapidly dialling some numbers.

'The lunch? Oh, *lunch* was all right. But I'm seriously beginning to wonder if that rotten man has got eyes in the back of his head,' Laura muttered darkly. 'It's either that or he's somehow managed to have my apartment bugged!'

'What on earth are you talking about?'

Laura gave a heavy sigh, almost slamming down the receiver when she could get no reply to her call.

'Jack Wilder—who can obviously see through walls!— has heard a rumour that Craig is thinking of leaving his agency and signing up with someone else.'

'So...?'

'So, while he obviously hasn't yet got enough information to actually *prove* that it's me who's trying to entice Craig from him, he gave me the gypsy's warning all the same.'

'But that's ridiculous!' Susie laughed. 'Why on earth would you want to have anything to do with Craig Jordan? We all know that you can't bear the man.'

'Mmm...I *was* rather relying on that fact to put everyone off the scent,' Laura admitted with a shrug. 'However, it's now beginning to look as though it was too much to expect Craig to keep his stupid mouth shut.'

'But...but why? Why take on Craig—of *all* people?' the other girl protested, almost unable to believe that Laura was being so incredibly foolish. 'Not only is he a *total* nightmare to deal with but he is also Jack's best, most highly paid client!'

'Which simply means that I'll have to work fast if I want to get him signed up before Jack discovers what I'm up to.'

Susie gave a heavy sigh and shook her head. 'Quite honestly, Laura, I think you must be completely out of your mind! Jack will never, *ever* forgive you if Craig signs up with this agency.' She agitatedly waved her hands in the air. 'Have you got a death-wish—or what?'

'I don't give *that* for Jack Wilder,' Laura told her with a derisory snap of her fingers. 'Besides, he's upset and treated *me* very badly—so why shouldn't he have a dose of his own medicine? Especially when I think about all that sweet-talk nonsense he was giving me during lunch. Believe me—the man's a real louse!'

Susie gave another heavy sigh. 'I can see that you're not going to take a blind bit of notice of anything I say. But it doesn't take a crystal ball to know that this is all going to end in tears.'

So, what else is new? Laura asked herself glumly. Having spent a good part of the past month weeping her heart out over Jack Wilder, what did a few more tears matter?

'By the way,' Susie told her, clearly deciding that her best course of action was to change the subject, 'I've had a call from Bill Chapman. He wants to know if we can provide one of our clients for a voice-over. It's for a big TV commercial due to be recorded next week.'

Laura shook her head. 'No, I'm sorry. Can you ring him back and make some excuse? Say our client's too busy—or whatever—but we may get back to him in the near future.'

'But why?' Her assistant frowned. 'Bill is offering part of the fee, and—'

'Because I had a really good idea last night, that's why!' Laura told her with a grin. 'I don't see any reason why I shouldn't set up my *own* voice-over business. I wouldn't set out to challenge any of the really big firms, of course, but I reckon that there's a real gap in the market for a small, specialised business.'

'You could be right...' Susie murmured, turning to gaze out of the window as she considered what Laura had just said. 'Bill seems to spend most of his time in the local pub, so you wouldn't have any problem in picking up some of his clients. In fact, they'd probably be grateful to do business with a more efficient firm like ours.'

'That's exactly what I thought,' Laura nodded. 'And I have to thank Jack for giving me the idea of a really *great* name for the new business. How does Sweet-Talk grab you?'

'Oh, my goodness! That...that's absolutely *brilliant*!' Susie gasped, before both girls dissolved into peals of almost hysterical laughter.

Laura leaned forward, opening the window of the taxi before slumping back against the hot leather seat.

This summer was proving to be a real scorcher! Day after day, the sun seemed to blaze down from a cloudless sky. Not having had any rain for the past three months, the city streets were hot and baking. And now, in the middle of July, both Laura and her assistant would have cheerfully given their eye-teeth for some air-conditioning in their glamorous offices.

However, apart from the fact that everyone in Britain appeared to be thoroughly fed up with the unexpected heatwave, Laura could at least look back over the past month with some satisfaction. Not only did it seem as if all her hard work was beginning to pay off at last, but her new voice-over business had really taken off in a big way. Bill Chapman wasn't at all happy about the situation, of course. However, as she'd told Susie, it served him right. 'How he ever hoped to run a successful business when he spent most of his time in the local bar beats me.'

Unfortunately, although many of her clients were doing really well, and achieving considerable success for her agency, Laura had been forced to acknowledge that she'd failed in one of her most important aims. Because Craig Jordan—living up to his well-known difficult and tricky character—had never bothered to return her phone calls. So she'd soon guessed that Craig had been using her as a stalking-horse—enabling him to genuinely claim that he was being head-hunted by another agency, in order to increase his bargaining power with Jack Wilder.

Well, that's life! Laura consoled herself now, brushing a weary hand through her hair. At least it was *one* quarrel which she'd avoided having with her ex-employer.

Not that she'd seen much of Jack over the past few weeks. In fact, her attempts to avoid all contact with him had proved to be highly successful. Unfortunately, however, there was little she could do to avoid seeing and reading about Jack in the Press. It seemed as though every time she picked up a newspaper Laura found herself gazing at a photograph of the handsome man, usually accompanied by his beautiful assistant, Felicity Green.

Apart from Christmas, it was the main time of year
for both film premières and charity functions. And since
Jack, as head of a successful theatrical agency, fre-
quently attended such shindigs it wasn't surprising that
he'd attracted the attention of press photographers. Especially when he had the delectable, amazingly curvaceous Miss Green on his arm.

Not that she gave a hoot one way or another, Laura
told herself firmly. In any case, there would have been
no point in *her* going to such functions, since she was
still in the process of working hard to establish her
agency. In fact, most of *her* time was spent either at
Agent Show evenings put on by the various drama
schools hoping to attract agents for their young actors,
or taking casting directors to view fringe plays in which
some of her new clients were displaying their talents.

It was hard, tiring but also rewarding work. Because
she was gradually building up a really solid list of good
actors who, over the next ten years or so, would start to
hit the big time.

Unfortunately, knowing that she was making all the
right moves businesswise was of little comfort as she
tossed and turned in her lonely bed night after night.
Because, if she was *really* honest, Laura knew that she'd
have given everything she possessed for a chance to take
the place of the ravishingly beautiful Felicity Green in
Jack's arms. Everyone in the theatrical business, of
course, seemed to be gossiping about the clearly obvious, torrid love affair between Jack and his new assistant. And you couldn't blame them, Laura thought
miserably. Not when they made such a spectacularly attractive couple.

Cut it out! That sort of thinking isn't going to do you any good at all, she told herself sternly as the taxi came to a halt outside her office building. Paying off the cab, and taking one last gulp of fresh air, she made her way across the foyer towards the bank of lifts.

'Come on!' she muttered under her breath, repeatedly punching the various buttons. But all to no avail. 'I'm fed up to the back teeth with these *grotty* lifts!' she yelled out loud, suddenly losing her temper and thumping her fist on the stainless-steel doors, which obstinately refused to open. 'If *somebody* doesn't do *something* about them, I'll... I'll...'

'Do what? Use a tin-opener?' an amused voice drawled sardonically from behind her rigidly angry figure.

'Ha-ha! *Very* funny!' she snapped, spinning around to glare up into Jack's eyes, which were gleaming with unconcealed mockery. 'If you're so damned clever why don't *you* try and get one of these beastly things to work?' she demanded, her fury increasing as she noticed his broad shoulders shaking with laughter.

And, of course, it was absolutely sickening to see the doors immediately fly open just as soon as he stepped forward to press the button. It was just one *more* reason to hate this man, Laura told herself furiously, not caring that she was being totally illogical and unreasonable in blaming Jack for the malfunction of the lifts. Studiously avoiding looking at him, she stared blindly down at the carpet as he joined her inside the small square steel cage.

Determined not to say anything for the few, short seconds she was forced to spend in his company, Laura was horrified when, after their initial upward 'whoosh', the lift came to a sudden grinding and shuddering halt.

'Oh, my God—we're *stuck*!' she cried, her voice echoing eerily around the confined space. 'For goodness' sake, Jack—do something!'

'Relax—there's no need to panic,' he murmured, opening a small square box beneath the controls and lifting out a phone. 'It happened to me twice last week,' he added, rapidly dialling a number. 'It's just a matter of keeping calm until help arrives.'

'I don't feel calm!' she gasped breathlessly, suddenly feeling as though the walls of the small space were somehow shrinking in towards her.

'Laura? Are you all right?'

Jack's voice seemed to be coming from a long way away. She could feel her head swimming and her legs becoming weak, as though they were going to collapse at any moment.

'It's OK, sweetheart. I'm here. You're going to be all right,' he said, moving quickly towards the girl slumped in the corner of the lift, who was gazing at him with blind, terrified green eyes, her face as white as a sheet. Clasping her quivering figure in his arms, he continued talking softly, rocking her gently back and forth as he would have comforted a frightened child.

'I'm so sorry...' she muttered helplessly, deeply thankful for the extraordinary feeling of warmth and safety engendered by the hard, strong arms about her trembling body. 'I don't know what's come over me... I don't usually... I mean, I've never had this sort of weird feeling before, and I really...'

'It's all right, sweetheart,' he told her quietly. 'I expect you're just suffering from a touch of claustrophobia, that's all.'

'But why...why can't the people who own this office block get their act together? Surely there *must* be a way to get these lifts working properly?' she moaned, burying her head in the curve of his shoulder, savouring the musky aroma of his cologne and desperately wishing that she could remain within the safety of his arms for ever.

'If you want action, maybe you'd better have a word with your friend Donald Hunt,' Jack murmured, grinning sardonically down at the girl in his arms, whose trembling figure had suddenly become stiff and rigid with alarm.

'D-Donald Hunt...?' she stuttered in a muffled voice, struggling to try and pull herself together. However, as she slowly raised her head and caught a glimpse of the unmistakably ironic, wry gleam in Jack's hooded grey eyes, Laura realised, with a sinking heart, that there was no point in trying to deceive him.

'You know about Donald...?' she breathed, completely forgetting the currently dangerous state of the lift as she waited helplessly for the expected storm to break over her confused and weary head.

However, she was surprised when Jack merely gave a low rumble of laughter. 'It was obvious you couldn't afford to set up an agency on your own. So it didn't take me very long to work out exactly *who* must be backing your new firm.'

'And...and you don't mind...?'

'Well, I wasn't exactly *thrilled* to discover that you were involved with my ex-partner,' Jack drawled sardonically. 'Nor to hear that he's virtually a fixture in your office. In fact, I'm told that Donald calls by practically every evening—no doubt to take you to dinner and nightclubs in his glamorous Rolls-Royce!' Jack added caustically.

'What?' Laura frowned, not having a clue what he was talking about. However, by the time she realised that he had obviously got his wires crossed, and didn't realise that it was *Susie* whom Donald was taking out practically every night, Jack had changed the subject.

'Although he's a very astute businessman, of course. So if Donald's backing you, then he must be quite confident that you're capable of being a success.'

'But I thought that you...that you and he...?'

Jack shook his dark head. 'Melissa and I both knew, within a few weeks of our marriage, that it had all been a ghastly mistake. I thought I was getting a wife—while she...' He hesitated for a moment, before giving a heavy sigh. 'Well, let's just say that Melissa was looking for a bigger step up the theatrical ladder than I could offer her at the time.

'Time is a great healer of problems, of course, and Melissa and I are now good friends. However, I obviously had to dissolve the partnership between Donald and myself—I could hardly, after all, keep on working closely with my wife's lover! But, in all fairness, I've never held him entirely to blame for what happened. Believe me, when Melissa *really* wants someone, or something, she's virtually unstoppable!' he added wryly as the lift gave another sudden lurch.

'*Help!*' she shrieked, closing her eyes and hanging onto Jack for dear life.

'Keep calm,' he told her firmly, his arms tightening about her once more. 'They've obviously got men working on the mechanism, and it won't be long before we're out of here. So what we must do is try and stop ourselves from thinking too much about the problem.'

Laura shuddered, ashamed of being so weak and feeble but now quite unable to think about *anything*—other than the fact that the lift might, any minute now, send them crashing down, out of control, towards the dark void far below.

'And he bent my ear about your new project.'

'What?' she muttered as Jack's strong, deep voice cut through the swirling mist of terror in her brain.

'I was just saying that I had Bill Chapman on the phone yesterday, belly-aching about your new voice-over business. That was a very bright idea, Laura. How's it going?'

'It...er...it's actually doing very well,' she murmured, relieved to find that when she shifted her weight slightly the lift remained rock-steady. 'As I told Susie the other day, it's no good Bill complaining that I've been pinching his business, because he's only got himself to blame,' she added in a stronger voice. 'That guy is so busy drinking his profits, he couldn't even run twenty yards—let alone a decent agency!'

Smiling down at the indignant figure in his arms, Jack was just congratulating himself on having successfully diverted Laura's mind from the danger they faced when he found himself wondering if it had been such a good idea after all.

'I'm glad you think it was a good idea,' she was saying, 'because I named my new business after you.'

'*What?*' His dark brows drawing quickly together in a deep frown, he gazed sternly down into her green eyes. 'Now *just* a minute!' he grated angrily. 'I've put up with about as much as I can stand from you, Laura. And if you think that I'm prepared to—'

'I was only joking,' she told him hurriedly. 'It was more an association of ideas—if you see what I mean.'

'No, I don't!' he growled. 'There's no way I'll allow you to use the name of my firm. Absolutely *no way*!'

'Hey—relax!' she protested. 'There's no need to go off the deep end. My new business has got *nothing* to do with either your name or your firm. In fact, I decided to call the new business Sweet-Talk, because it's both a pun on voice-overs and because sweet-talk is what I've mostly had from you—you foul man!'

There were both surprised when, after staring down at her blankly for a moment, Jack found himself giving a reluctant bark of laughter.

'You are, without doubt, the most impossible female I've *ever* had the misfortune to meet!' he told her sternly, despite the fact that his hooded grey eyes were gleaming with amusement. 'Which reminds me,' he added blandly. 'I thought you'd like to know that Craig Jordan has signed a new contract with me.'

'I'm not surprised,' Laura shrugged.

'But you *did* try to get him to join your new agency, didn't you?'

She hesitated for some moments. 'Well, yes, you're right—I did,' she admitted at last. 'I never had any real hope that he'd sign up with me, of course. But I reckoned it was worth a try.'

'It certainly would have been—if you'd managed to pull it off,' he agreed grimly. 'However, don't *ever* again make the mistake of trying to poach one of my major clients. Because if you do I'll come down on you like a ton of bricks. I'm not kidding, Laura,' he added, his voice heavy with menace. 'I've got a lot of clout in the theatrical business, and I can promise to make you wish that you'd never been born!'

'OK, OK...I've got the message,' she muttered, her cheeks flaming as she stared fixedly down at the blue and red pattern on his tie. 'What's Craig doing at the moment?' she asked, more to break the strained silence than because of any real desire to know more about the difficult and neurotic film star.

'Nothing particularly exciting.' Jack shrugged. 'Although we've one or two things in the pipeline, of course.'

After wrestling with her conscience—which was telling her in a loud, incessant voice that Jack really *had* been remarkably tolerant and forgiving over her attempt to steal one of his major clients—Laura knew that she really did owe him a favour.

'I...er...I think I might have a useful contact for you,' she said, and explained about the film deal she'd been hoping to put together. 'I hate to say it, but there's no doubt that Craig would be absolutely *perfect* for the role of Macbeth.'

'You're right—he would!' Jack grinned.

'So why don't you put him forward for the part? If it's any help, I can easily set up a meeting with the producer—and you can take it from there.'

'Well, it sounds all right,' he murmured, his voice heavy with doubt. 'But, since you're putting this idea forward, I find myself wondering just what's the catch.'

'There's *no* damn catch! Can't I at least do *something* right once in a while?' she cried, quickly twisting herself from his loose embrace and turning her back on the hateful man as she leaned her hot forehead against the cool, shiny steel wall of the lift.

'Oh, sweetheart—I'm sorry,' he murmured, staring at the girl's dejected figure, only a foot or so away from his own.

'I'm fed up with this continual sniping at one another,' she muttered tearfully. 'I wish to goodness that I'd never had the idea of starting my own agency.'

'I wish you hadn't as well!' he agreed with a low rumble of laughter, taking a step forward and slipping his hands around her waist. 'But that's just sour grapes on my part. Because there's no doubt that everyone is talking about Laura Parker's successful new agency!'

'Really?'

'Mmm…really,' he murmured, pulling her slowly back against his hard body.

'No, Jack—please! Don't do this to me,' she protested huskily as he lowered his head to press a kiss on the long, slim line of her neck.

But she was so hungry for his touch that she couldn't prevent herself from involuntarily shivering with excitement as his hands began moving over her soft curves, before slowly undoing the buttons of her sleeveless dark blue dress; nor could she prevent a trembling response to his sharp intake of breath as he discovered that, due to the heat, she wasn't wearing a bra.

'You're so lovely,' he muttered thickly, swiftly opening her dress to the waist and allowing his hands to roam freely as he savoured the pleasure of her taut, firm breasts, his fingers brushing over their hard, swollen peaks—an intimate touch which produced an instantaneous, deep clenching of the muscles in her stomach, and caused her to groan with passion and desire.

It was as if her helpless moans, echoing around the confined space, acted as a trigger for his own emotional response. Quickly spinning her around, he roughly crushed her soft, yielding body in a fierce embrace. Lowering his dark head, he possessed her lips in a kiss of scorching intensity, the urgent thrust of his tongue driving her almost wild with desire.

While one part of her mind was utterly appalled that she could be behaving in such a totally abandoned, wanton manner, the other seemed completely deaf to anything other than the wild clamour of sensual excitement swirling erotically through her veins. There was nothing she wanted more in the whole, wide world than to feel this man's hard, aroused body pressed tightly to her own; to revel in the knowledge of the sheer naked lust and passion which always seemed to be sparked into a raging fire whenever they were alone together.

Laura never knew whether she *would* have become completely lost to all sense, and allowed herself to succumb to his increasingly urgent lovemaking. Because, before they reached the point of no return, they became aware of the shiny steel box being jerkily lifted upwards.

Their ears filled with muffled cries of encouragement and promises of their early release, Laura and Jack stared at each other in horror, then quickly and hurriedly adjusted their clothing.

'Don't worry, sweetheart,' he murmured, swiftly brushing aside her nervously shaking fingers and pressing a warm kiss on the deep valley between her breasts, before quickly doing up the buttons of her dress. 'I'll make sure that I cause a terrific fuss and rumpus, which will give you time to slink quietly away to your office.'

'Slink away' just about summed up the whole story of their relationship, she told herself wearily, suddenly feeling cold and miserably unhappy at the thought of just how easily—and how stupidly—she'd once more been betrayed by her feelings for this man.

Closing her eyes, Laura leaned back against the steel wall, vowing never to let herself get into such a position ever again. Because she most definitely was *not* one of those people who either enjoyed or got their kicks from making love in strange and public places. Neither was she someone who would enjoy living the unhappy, ultimately frustrating secret life of a kept mistress.

As the men outside were busy trying to crowbar open the lift door, Laura realised that there was nothing she could do to stop herself from loving this impossible man. But, if she was forced to tell the truth, she'd have to admit that she wanted all those supposedly boring, mundane things—such as marrying Jack, and creating a warm, loving home in which to bring up their children.

Unfortunately, it was clear that a happily married life was not one of Jack's aims or ambitions. So it wasn't too difficult to draw the obvious conclusion that the sooner she cut him ruthlessly away from her life and refused to have anything more to do with him the better.

CHAPTER SEVEN

LAURA put down the script for a TV comedy series and turned to gaze out of the train window. There was no way she'd put forward any of *her* clients for the new series. It was really awful—almost as dull and boring as the weather, she told herself glumly, hardly able to view the passing scenery for the torrential rain pelting down from a grey, leaden sky.

Following the long heatwave, when everyone in Britain had become heartily tired of the sun blazing down day after day, their prayers for release had finally been answered by a violent thunderstorm. Unfortunately, the welcome break had only led to dreary weeks of seemingly never-ending, continuous rain. And, whereas only a month ago the Press had been full of tales of severe drought, and the need to carefully ration water supplies, newspapers now carried reports of coastal erosion, rivers flooding their banks, and occasional grim references to Noah and his Ark.

It's all Jack's fault! she grumbled to herself, not caring if she was being totally unreasonable. While she couldn't, of course, blame him for the vile weather, Laura had no doubt that just about everything else which had happened to her lately stemmed from her disastrous relationship with Jack Wilder. Except . . . well, maybe all those problems with the film production company couldn't be laid at his door.

However, if Jack hadn't been Craig's agent, and also once married to that highly temperamental actress Melissa Grant, Laura was quite certain that she wouldn't have been dragged into the current mess. And it certainly *was* his fault that she'd been woken up at the unearthly hour of six this morning and forced to cancel everything at a moment's notice, before scrambling to catch this train to a remote area of the Northumberland coast.

Following her encounter with Jack in the lift—the memory of which could still make her go hot and cold with embarrassment all these weeks later—Laura had done her very best to make sure that she avoided all sight and sound of the man who'd cast such a blight over her life. And she might have succeeded in finally rooting all trace of him from her existence if she hadn't felt obliged to follow through on the offer she'd made to contact the producer of the *Macbeth* film and set up a meeting between him and Jack.

After keeping her word, she'd thought no more about it, until she'd arrived in the office one morning to find a *huge* bouquet of red roses from Jack—together with a card expressing his thanks, and the news that Craig had been given the part of Macbeth.

That might well have been that if, only a few days later, she hadn't been startled to hear that Melissa Grant was in the outside office and wondering if she could have a word.

'Are you quite sure...?' Laura had frowned in puzzlement. 'I mean, why on earth would Melissa Grant want to see *me*?'

'I haven't a clue,' Susie had shrugged. 'However, there's no doubt that it is you she wants to see. In fact, she declared that she's quite prepared to wait—all day, if necessary—until you can find time to see her.'

It was such an extraordinary statement that Laura had gazed at her assistant in open-mouthed astonishment. Melissa Grant, that well-known and highly successful actress, wouldn't normally wait to see *anyone*—let alone the owner of a small theatrical agency.

'Good heavens!' Laura had exclaimed, leaning back in her chair and shaking her head with amazement. 'Well, you'd better wheel her in,' she'd told Susie with a grin.

Taken completely aback by Melissa's unexpected arrival in her office, Laura had had no time to think about how she would feel at meeting Jack's ex-wife for the first time. In the event, she'd been surprised to discover that she hadn't, as she might have supposed, suffered from the sharp, clawing pangs of jealousy.

Even thinking later about her reaction to the outstandingly lovely woman, Laura hadn't been able to decide if it had been simply because Melissa was *so* beautiful and it was clearly a pure waste of time to envy her looks, or whether it had been because—against all the odds—she'd found herself unexpectedly amused and intrigued by someone who appeared to be so amazingly self-centred.

It hadn't been difficult to see why the famous star had caused such a sensation over the years, both on the stage and in her private life. A well-known theatre critic had once described this woman, elegantly seated on a chair in front of Laura's desk, as 'embodying all my sexual fantasies of the deliciously wicked Queen Jezebel'. Leaving aside the possible slur on her character, there was no doubt that with those enormous, cat-like amber eyes set over pale alabaster cheeks and her long, smooth hair, the shimmering blue-black colour of raven's wings, twisted in a heavy chignon at the base of her swan-like neck, Melíssa Grant really was exquisitely lovely.

However, by the end of the interview, Laura had come to the conclusion that both the critic and Jack Wilder had been quite right. Melissa might well be stunningly beautiful—as well as exuding an obviously heady aroma of rampant sex appeal—but when Jack's ex-wife decided that she wanted someone, or something, she clearly wasn't prepared to let anyone stand in her way.

The meeting had, in fact, started off in an easy and relaxed fashion, with the older woman paying Laura many compliments on having the courage to open her own agency, and to have made a success of it in such a small space of time. It had only been afterwards that Laura had realised she'd been a victim of both Melissa's fatal charm and her outstanding talent for manipulating others to her will.

'The thing is, darling, I've got a small problem at the moment,' she said at last, after Susie had brought them both a cup of coffee. 'I'm rather fed up with the agent who's currently looking after my career. I can't help feeling that I could do *far* better with someone who's young and enthusiastic, if you see what I mean? Which is why I've come to see you, darling.'

'Me?' Laura muttered, trying not to look too flabbergasted at the idea that she, a virtual newcomer to the profession, could be of any use to such a famous actress. 'You don't mean . . . ?'

'Yes, of course, darling,' Melissa purred with a dazzling smile. 'I hear that you've got some *wonderful* contacts—not to mention several useful friends in high places! So I'm quite sure that you'd look after me really, really well.'

Trying to control a fast-rising tide of excitement and exhilaration at the prospect of signing up such a well-known star, Laura strove to be as businesslike as possible.

'I'd obviously be delighted to have you join my agency,' she told Melissa with a broad grin. 'But there are one or two important points to sort out straight away. For instance, I need to know what plans you may already have for the future. I'm assuming,' she added, pulling a pad of paper towards her, 'that you'll be starring in your present long-running play for some months ahead?'

Melissa shrugged her delicate, slim shoulders. 'Well, the thing is, darling, I'm not really sure *what* I'm going to do. It's all a bit complicated. But maybe if I put you in the picture you'll be able to find a way to help little old me?'

A few minutes later, leaning back in her chair while Melissa sipped her cup of coffee, Laura stared down at the notes in front of her. Stripped of all the 'darlings', and several cloying references to 'little old me', it seemed that Melissa had an opportunity, during the next two weeks, to take advantage of a break clause in her contract with the theatre management. This would allow her to leave the successful production whose seats were sold out for months ahead. But obviously Melissa would only do so if she had a more exciting and challenging role on the horizon. And it was the prospect of one particular part which had brought her to Laura's agency.

'The thing is, darling, I'm just madly, *madly* in love! It's definitely the *real thing* this time!' Melissa declared happily, conveniently forgetting her past track record of some five husbands—not to mention innumerable lovers.

And when she announced that the current love of her life was Laura's least favourite actor, Craig Jordan, it was all the younger girl could do not to groan out loud. Not only was Craig at least ten years younger than Melissa, but he was completely incapable of being faithful to one woman for more than a few weeks at a time. So there could only be one result of this relationship—which was clearly doomed from the start.

'I hear that you've helped to find my darling Craig such a *wonderful* part in that new film. So I'm sure that you can find one for me too,' Melissa trilled in her bell-like voice. 'Quite honestly, darling, I've *always* wanted to play Lady Macbeth. I really do think that it's absolutely *my* role—don't you?'

'Oh, *absolutely*!' Laura echoed, wondering how on earth she was managing to keep a straight face. Craig—who'd happily double-cross anyone to get his own way—was perfect casting for the part of the deeply conniving, ambitious Thane of Cawdor. And, now she came to think about it, who better than Melissa—certainly as far as looks and talent were concerned—to play the role of his equally ambitious, evil wife?

'You'd be wonderful in the part,' Laura agreed. 'There's only one problem. The role has already been offered to a well-known American actress, and I really don't see how—'

'Please! I *really* don't want to hear any of these negative comments,' Melissa said firmly, a hard, threatening note appearing in her voice for the first time during their interview. 'I mean, it's all very simple, darling. If you want me to sign up with your agency, you're going to get me the part of Lady Macbeth. I'm *quite* sure you can do it,' she added, with a determined glint in her feline eyes. 'After all, you *do* want to be my new agent, don't you, darling?'

'Phew!' Susie breathed after Melissa had swept out of the office and she'd been put in the picture by Laura. 'If you can sign up Melissa Grant, this agency is well and truly made!' she added excitedly. 'Everyone, but *everyone*, will be mad keen to join us once they know Melissa's come on board!'

'Hey—calm down!' Laura warned. 'There's no point in getting too excited about the prospect of attracting such a well-known client. While I may have been instrumental in getting Craig a starring role in the film, my chances of doing the same for his new girlfriend are just about zilch. So unfortunately I think that's the last we're likely to see of Melissa Grant.'

However, despite her dire warning, Laura didn't reckon on the fickle finger of fate taking a hand in the affair.

Either Melissa was just born lucky or she'd managed to cast a transatlantic evil eye on the American film star, who'd been due to fly to England to begin filming the following week. Because hard on the heels of her interview with Melissa came the news that the American actress had been forced to withdraw in order to nurse her husband, a well-known photographer, who'd been suddenly rushed to hospital following a massive heart attack.

'I wish to heaven that I'd *never* got involved with this film!' the producer moaned to Laura, when she contacted him following the news of the latest disaster to hit the production. 'I now see exactly *why* everyone in the theatrical profession has always regarded the play as being so desperately unlucky.'

'I'm sorry to hear about all your problems, of course,' Laura told him sympathetically. 'However, it just so happens that I might be able to suggest a solution.' When she'd explained the possibility of being able to provide him with a replacement—and not just any actress, but Melissa Grant herself—he was over the moon.

'Bless you, darling!' he cried, his relief almost tangible over the phone. 'First Craig—and now Melissa! Is there *anyone* you can't get hold of?' he added with a laugh.

Only the man I love with all my heart, she thought unhappily as she put down the phone. However, since there was absolutely no point in torturing herself any further over Jack Wilder, she pulled herself together and telephoned Melissa to tell her the good news.

Laura wouldn't have been entirely surprised if, on gaining the coveted part, Melissa had reneged on the promise she'd made to join the agency. However, the actress kept her word, and after happily signing a contract with Laura she packed her bags before joining Craig and the rest of the film crew on location in the far north of England.

And there, once again, the matter might well have rested, with Laura being left in peace to concentrate on her own business. But unfortunately she soon found herself echoing the film producer's plaintive wails about what was clearly a doomed film.

The first intimation of fresh trouble in store came in a phone call from Jack himself.

'You'd better get yourself up here as soon as you can,' he said, sounding thoroughly harassed and quite unlike his normally smooth, confident self. 'Thanks to the ghastly weather, most of the film crew found themselves practically washed out to sea near Lindisfarne, so the set is being relocated to an old Gothic castle a few miles south of here.'

'So? I don't see what all this has to do with me,' she muttered, busy gathering the papers on her desk in front of her and glancing anxiously down at her watch. She was already late for a lunch date with an important casting director, who wouldn't be at all pleased to be kept waiting. 'I can't think why you've got yourself involved. Surely the film company can sort out their own problems?'

'I've been dragged up here because Craig and Melissa have had a violent lovers' quarrel and are no longer talking to one another,' he told her, his voice heavy with irritation and annoyance.

'Well, I'm sure you can sort it out without my help,' she retorted, before putting down the phone and hurrying out of her office.

'I thought I told you *not* to put through any more calls from Jack Wilder?' she said to Susie on returning from what had been a successful lunch. 'Didn't I make it crystal-clear that I don't want to have *anything* to do with him?'

'Yes, well...' Susie looked at her sheepishly. 'Jack was very insistent and seemed genuinely anxious to get hold of you, so...'

'OK, OK.' Laura gritted her teeth and took a deep breath. 'I know he's an attractive man. I know he can be *very* persuasive. But, as far as I'm concerned, he's nothing but trouble with a capital T. So why don't you type out a nice, large notice that says ''Laura Parker doesn't take calls from Jack Wilder'' and stick it up on the wall, where you just might have a chance of seeing it?' she added grimly, before marching into her own office and slamming the door loudly behind her.

It didn't, of course, take her many minutes to simmer down and realise that she'd behaved very badly. Ashamed of having been so rude to her assistant, she walked back into Susie's office.

'I'm sorry. There was no excuse for being so nasty and aggressive,' she told the other girl in a penitent voice. 'It's just that...'

'It's just that the path of true love is proving to be a rocky and stony one?' Susie completed the sentence with a wry smile.

Laura sighed. 'Well, you're right about the rocks and stones. Every time I think I've finally managed to get that man out of my hair, something comes up which blows all my good resolutions to smithereens. But I'm going to keep on trying,' she added, with another heavy sigh. 'And maybe, if I get *really* lucky, one of these days I'm finally going to succeed.'

The path of true love—that's a joke! Laura told herself once she was back in her own office. As far as she could see, there was no path and absolutely *no* true love—on Jack Wilder's side, anyway. Mr Loverman was only interested in one very short, three-letter word: sex. And, since *his* copy of the dictionary obviously didn't contain such words as 'love' and 'commitment', Laura knew that she was absolutely right to insist on having nothing to do with such a handsome, lethally attractive man.

Unfortunately, Jack obviously came a close second to his ex-wife, Melissa, when pursuing an objective. She ought to have known that he wouldn't give up, she told herself now, staring blindly out of the train window at grey, rain-lashed, desolate moorland. Balked and frustrated in his attempts to contact Laura at the office, the swine hadn't hesitated to ring her at home.

'For heaven's sake, Jack!' she'd muttered, when roused from a deep sleep at the ridiculously early hour of six o'clock this morning.

'Wake up, Laura, we've got some important matters to discuss.'

'You must be kidding! It's practically the middle of the night,' she'd protested, struggling to sit up in bed as she brushed the tousled hair from her eyes.

'Nonsense! I and most of the crew have been on set since five-thirty. But that's not important,' he'd added impatiently. 'We've got real problems here, and they mostly centre on your new client, Melissa Grant.'

'She may be my client but she's *your* ex-wife!' Laura had retorted grimly. 'So if there are any problems I'm quite sure you're by far the best person to sort them out.'

Jack had given a heavy sigh. 'Melissa never listened to me in the past—and she *certainly* isn't listening to me now,' he'd admitted in a quieter tone of voice. 'The situation we're facing is that your client has locked herself in her hotel room and is refusing to come out. On top of which, Craig is also proving to be a complete nightmare.'

'So, what else is new?'

'Neither of the two principals involved are willing to talk to one another, let alone act the parts for which they are being paid a large fee,' he'd continued, ignoring her cynical interjection. 'So you're going to have to get up here as soon as possible and help me sort out this mess.'

'Forget it! I can't possibly drop everything and—'

'Oh, yes, you can,' he'd snapped. 'Before you say anything else, my dear Laura, I'd better point out one or two nasty facts,' he'd added grimly. 'If Melissa continues to act in such a thoroughly unprofessional manner, she'll never be offered another part in a film. The second point is that if we don't do something to resolve the problem this film is going down the tubes. And *if* that happens the film company are likely to sue both Craig and Melissa for the loss of all potential earnings.'

'What rubbish! That's hardly what I'd call a likely scenario.'

'Oh, really?' he'd drawled. 'Well, you may feel like taking a chance on the film's financiers happily waving goodbye to a few million pounds but *I* wouldn't like to bet on it!'

Laura had bitten her lip. Jack was bound to be exaggerating the problem, of course. But... all the same... she couldn't possibly just stand by and allow Melissa to commit professional suicide.

'Well?' he demanded. 'Have you got the message at last?'

'Yes—message received and understood,' Laura had sighed, throwing off the bedclothes and swinging her feet to the floor, yawning sleepily as she searched amongst the objects on her bedside table for a pen and paper. 'Give me directions on where and how to meet you and I'll get there as soon as I can.'

Which was how she now found herself on a train, speeding towards the far north-east of England. Although why the director of the film should have decided to do location shots on the coast of Northumberland and not in Scotland—where, of course, the story of Macbeth had originally been set—was completely beyond her. However, she was keeping her fingers crossed and hoping that this train really *was* going to stop at a small railway station near Alnwick, and not carry her on to its ultimate destination on the other side of the border, in Edinburgh.

'You took your time,' Jack muttered some time later, leading her swiftly from the station to where he'd parked his car.

'Kindly direct your complaints to British Rail,' she retorted as he helped her into the passenger seat of the large, comfortably warm car, before walking round to slide in behind the wheel. 'I only managed to catch the train from King's Cross this morning by the skin of my teeth, I had to change trains at Newcastle upon Tyne, nor have I had anything to eat since late last night. When I'm hungry I'm also likely to be extremely bad-tempered. So don't push your luck!' she added grimly.

'Relax, sweetheart!'

'And *don't* call me "sweetheart", either!' she ground out through clenched teeth.

'Why not? You know we're crazy about each other.'

'I know nothing of the sort!' she snapped, glaring at the man, whose grey eyes were gleaming with amusement. 'And you can stop laughing,' she added bitterly. 'Believe me, there's nothing funny about a man who is expecting his *ex*-girlfriend to sort out his *ex*-wife's problems. In fact, this whole business is...well, it's totally *bizarre*!'

'That's my girl!' he drawled wryly. 'She may be hungry, cold and tired—but, my God, she still packs a hefty verbal punch! However,' he added with a grin, 'I suggest that we put aside the vexed question of Melissa for a moment and concentrate on giving you something to eat.'

Twisting in his seat, he lifted a small wicker basket from the seat and placed it on her lap. 'I thought you might be hungry. So I had the inn where I'm staying make up a picnic for you. They promised to include a Thermos of hot coffee and some ham sandwiches.'

'Mmm... thanks, Jack—this is wonderful!' Laura muttered some minutes later, beginning to feel at least partly human for the first time that day.

'More coffee?'

She nodded, not caring that he was grinning at her as she wolfed down the last of the sandwiches. 'Tell me,' she said at last, 'why on earth are they shooting this film here, on the Northumberland coast, and not in the Highlands of Scotland, with all those wonderful castles to choose from?'

Jack shrugged his broad shoulders. 'I've no idea,' he confessed. 'However, it seems the director of the film, George Davidson, grew up in these parts and has always wanted to set a film on this bleak, ruggedly wild coastline. I must say,' he added reflectively, 'the castle he's now chosen certainly looks very dramatic. In fact, providing we can get Melissa and Craig to behave, this film could be a smash hit.'

'OK,' she sighed as he packed up the wicker picnic basket, then tossed it onto the back seat. 'That sounds like a cue for me to get back to work. So I think you'd better fill me in on everything that's happened so far.'

'Oh, nothing particularly surprising or unusual as far as neurotic, temperamental film stars are concerned,' he told her with a cynical smile as he turned the key in the ignition. 'Just an everyday mixture of star-crossed lovers, high drama and raving hysterics!'

Jack drove carefully along the narrow country roads until they reached the A1, when the large, comfortable car moved smoothly into the fast traffic streaming north.

Leaning back in the comfortable passenger seat and enjoying the expensive, luxurious scent of the cream leather upholstery, Laura closed her eyes for a minute, feeling sleepy and replete. She knew that she was going to regret answering Jack's SOS—even if it involved trying to save Melissa Grant's professional reputation. But, just at the moment, she didn't care.

Deeply conscious of the lean, muscled body sitting beside her, and the slim, tanned fingers resting confidently on the wheel, she realised that she was, at long last, feeling happy and content for the first time in many weeks. Jack might be totally infuriating, and regularly drive her up the wall. But he was also a devastatingly attractive, exciting and amusing man—with whom she was deeply in love.

And, even though she knew that having anything more to do with him could only end in tears and profound unhappiness, she was helpless to resist the overwhelming impact of those gleaming grey eyes and that long, hard body on her weak and fragile heart.

'Wake up, Laura!'

'Hmm...?' She blinked her heavy lids, gazing foggily up at the handsome face leaning over her.

'It's all right. You were obviously tired, so I thought I'd let you sleep till we got here,' Jack told her, gently brushing a stray lock of hair from her face.

'Ugh...I feel awful,' she muttered, yawning as she gazed out of the car window. 'I don't know where the heck we are—but at least it seems to have stopped raining,' she added, before yawning again and wishing that she didn't feel quite so thick in the head.

He got out of the car and came around to open her door. 'Come on—I'm sure you could do with some fresh air.'

'I suppose so,' she agreed, undoing her seat belt and letting him help her out onto the damp, springy green turf.

A moment later, she was almost knocked off her feet by a rough gust of wind. Indeed, if Jack hadn't still had his hand firmly on her arm, she was almost sure that she would have been blown over the high, bleak clifftop and down onto the pale sandy beach far below.

'I've heard of fresh air,' she gasped, 'but this is ridiculous!'

'Careful,' he warned, putting his arm about her waist and holding her closely against him. 'It's a steep drop from here, but I wanted you to see this fabulous view.'

'Oh, *heavens*!' she breathed as he turned her to face the huge, turreted stone castle, situated on a craggy rock peninsula which jutted out into the sea. Surrounded on three sides by turbulent waves, crashing loudly against the jagged grey rocks, it was a spectacular and amazing sight.

'Isn't it fantastic?' Jack shouted against the wind battering their two figures. 'You can see why George Davidson was so keen to use this castle for his location shots.'

'Absolutely!' she yelled back, shivering at the cold blasts of air from the sea and thankful for the protective warmth and shelter of Jack's tall, broad-shouldered figure as he led her back to the car.

'More coffee? You must have taken up clairvoyance in your old age!' she grinned, when they were back inside the vehicle and Jack had produced, like a conjuror's rabbit from a top hat, another Thermos of steaming hot coffee.

He laughed. 'We'll have less of the "old" if you don't mind! Although I do feel as though I've aged a few years during the past week,' he added in a wry drawl. 'Normally dealing with either Craig or Melissa is enough to drive anyone up the wall. But together...' He shook his dark head ruefully. 'I can tell you that it's an explosive mixture of unstable TNT.'

'But that's the point I was trying to make before you hauled me up here from London.' She shrugged. 'Leaving the question of Craig aside for the moment, I don't understand why you seem to think that I can solve Melissa's problems. If *you* can't cope with your ex-wife— who, besides being spectacularly beautiful, also strikes me as being totally self-centred and as stubborn as a mule—I don't reckon that I'm going to have much luck either!'

'Well, I was hoping that maybe a bit of female solidarity might work—because, God knows, we've tried everything else,' he admitted with a sigh. 'I'm sorry that you've found yourself dragged into this mess.'

'But I still don't see...'

'Look—let's just get one or two things straight,' he said sharply. 'I may have once been married to Melissa, but we were both *very* young—she was just eighteen, I was twenty-two—and our so-called "marriage" only lasted a few months. The failure was probably as much my fault as hers, since I was a total workaholic, and not prepared to give Melissa either the time or the attention she obviously needed.

'However—' he shrugged '—I'm now thirty-eight. I've had plenty of time in which to regret having been such a fool as to wed a woman simply because she was stunningly good-looking. If and when we bump into each other nowadays, it's...well, I suppose it's rather like meeting an old acquaintance—someone you knew vaguely in the past but who has nothing to do with your present-day existence.

'On the other hand,' he continued as Laura remained silent, quietly sipping her coffee, 'when I heard you'd taken on Melissa as a client, I nearly had a heart attack! *Not*, I can assure you, because of any tender feelings for my ex-wife,' he explained with a dry smile. 'But I knew that she couldn't have changed all that much over the years. And, while she is a great actress, with an even more glittering future ahead of her, she's also extraordinarily difficult—with a very low threshold of boredom. In fact, I was quite certain that this time, Laura, you'd *really* bitten off more than you could chew!'

'Mmm...it's beginning to look as if you could be right,' she agreed slowly, impressed that he had been so honest about his own possible contribution to the breakdown of the marriage, and also with Jack's generosity in praising his pesky ex-wife. 'All the same, Melissa really *is* very talented, isn't she?'

He quickly nodded his dark head. 'Oh, yes. There's absolutely no doubt about that. I've seen the rushes from the first few days' filming—before the balloon went up, of course—and she really lights up the screen. Which is why it's so important to try and get her back on the set.'

'What caused the trouble in the first place?'

'Craig, of course!' Jack's lips tightened with annoyance. 'You'd think the stupid man could manage to stay faithful to his new love for a few days at least. But oh, no! Apparently, as soon as he got up here he began a rip-roaring affair with one of the make-up girls.'

'Just to make sure there was no slip-up with *his* appearance on film...?' she enquired cynically.

'I shouldn't be at all surprised,' Jack agreed, with a snort of grim laughter. 'However, the upshot was that Melissa, after having been up here for a few days, discovered Craig and the girl in the process of making love. I'm told the explosion that followed was of atomic proportions—and the two principals haven't exchanged one word from that day to this!'

In the silence that followed, Laura took a final sip of coffee, before placing her cup on the dashboard and leaning back in her seat, buried in thought as she stared blindly through the windscreen.

'I wasn't joking about this situation being quite extraordinarily bizarre,' she said at last, with a heavy sigh. 'We're both involved in show business, which can be a very unreal world at the best of times, with the most outrageous things being regarded as quite normal. But, while I like to think that I'm a reasonably sophisticated woman, the tangled web of your relationship with Melissa, and hers with Craig—coupled with raving histrionics and over-the-top melodrama—goes well beyond *anything* I've ever had to cope with before now.'

'I'm sorry, sweetheart.' He shifted in his seat as he turned to face her. 'Unfortunately, once you succumbed to the temptation of having Melissa on your books, this sort of thing was bound to happen sooner or later.

However, I'm quite sure that you'll be able to sort out the problem.'

Laura shook her head. 'No, I really don't think I can. I mean...' She swallowed nervously, all her senses suddenly alert to the dangerous, dynamic masculinity of this man now leaning so close to her.

The problems of Craig and Melissa were nothing when compared to her own complicated, intense relationship with her ex-employer. Why was it that when discussing basic, down-to-earth theatrical or agency matters she didn't have too much of a problem in temporarily suppressing her feelings and dealing with the business in hand, but as soon as Jack turned those gleaming, hooded grey eyes in her direction she...well, she just seemed to go to pieces?

'You can do it, sweetheart,' he murmured, leaning so close that she could almost feel the persuasive energy emanating from his hard, broad-shouldered body. So close that the aromatic scent of his cologne filled her nostrils, his breath fanning her cheek as she stared, mesmerised, up at the mouth just above her own, a sick and trembling excitement running like liquid fire through her veins.

'No....no, I really can't...' she breathed, her husky protest dying away as his dark head came down towards her, his mouth slowly and softly seducing her lips apart. His hands slipped inside her open coat, sliding over her soft cashmere sweater to caress her breasts. His intimate and sensual touch, like a match thrown into a barrel of gasoline, sent desire flaring like a raging inferno deep inside her. Gasping helplessly beneath his warm lips, she was left feeling desperately bereft as he slowly and reluctantly raised his head.

As they stared at each other in a long silence that seemed to last for ever, Laura tried to pull her distraught mind together. But she was only aware of the heavy pounding of his heart and the faint flush beneath the tanned skin of his high cheekbones.

'This is nothing but... but emotional blackmail!' she gasped, wincing at the sound of her own rough, ragged breathing as it seemed to echo loudly within the confined space.

'But you *will* help me sort out the mess—won't you, sweetheart?' he murmured, raising his hands to gently frame her face, his lips hovering tantalisingly over her own. 'Just this once, hmm...?'

'Oh, Jack...' she moaned, knowing that she was a fool and completely out of her mind, but hopelessly beguiled and trapped, like a fly in a spider's web, as he enticingly brushed his warm lips over her soft, trembling mouth. 'Well... maybe... just this once...'

CHAPTER EIGHT

'OK, MELISSA, let's take it one more time from the top, shall we? Are you prepared to go back to work tomorrow morning?'

Laura sighed heavily as she waited for the woman to answer the fairly simple question. But, with this beautiful actress—now dramatically striding about the room, with her cloud of long black hair flowing down over a crimson brocade robe—*nothing* was either straightforward or simple.

Melissa would, without a doubt, try the patience of a saint! She'd certainly managed to antagonise just about the whole film crew. The director, George Davidson, had merely thrown up his hands in disgust before walking off the set, but the two co-producers were desperately trying to keep the news of Craig and Melissa's quarrel out of the newspapers. Because once the Press got wind of what was happening the financial backers of the film were likely to become understandably nervous.

'I don't care *what* you do,' George Davidson had told Laura tersely, when Jack had taken her to meet the director. 'Promise her the earth, if you think it will work. But unless Melissa is on the set first thing tomorrow morning I'm going to give her the sack!' he'd added sternly, before turning to her companion.

'And the same goes for *your* client too, Jack. I'm sorry to have to do this, because you're one of the few people I respect in this crazy industry,' he'd continued, with a

weary shrug. 'However, while Craig Jordan may think
he's got a great career in films, I'm holding him chiefly
to blame for this current crisis. So just make sure he
understands that if he *isn't* on set tomorrow I'll make
damn sure that he has a very rough time getting any
more work. In fact,' he added grimly, 'when *my* version
of what's happened hits the news-stands, dear Craig is
going to wish that he'd never been born!'

Leaving Jack to read the Riot Act to his client, Laura
had gone to Melissa's hotel. It hadn't been easy even
persuading the actress to let her into the large bedroom
suite. Then, having gained admittance at last, she'd been
forced to listen to a dramatic monologue in which Melissa
acted out the whole, involved scenario leading to her
discovery of Craig's infidelity. This somewhat muddled
and hysterical rendition had also included a considerable amount of bitchy, malicious references to some
of her previous husbands.

However, glancing down at her watch, and noting that
she'd had to listen to this nonsense for well over an hour,
Laura had finally lost her temper.

'OK—that's quite enough!' she'd said loudly, cutting
Melissa off in full flow. 'Craig may well be a rotten swine
who deserves a fate worse than death. But I actually
don't care about that at the moment. Because if you
don't get your act together, *tout de suite*, Craig is going
to be the very *least* of your problems.'

'But you don't understand...' Melissa had moaned,
throwing herself dramatically down onto the bed. 'My
life is ruined, and—'

'You're dead right!' Laura had agreed grimly. 'If
you're not on set first thing tomorrow morning, George
Davidson is going to have you thrown off this film.

Everyone is going to blame you for what's happened. The newspapers will have a field-day. And you'll have the devil's own job getting *any* work, ever again.'

'They... they can't *do* this to me!' Melissa had gasped in horror.

Laura had given a harsh laugh. 'No? Well, I've got news for you, *darling*. They can—and they will! Yes, I know it's mostly Craig's fault,' she retorted impatiently over the other woman's loud protests. 'But so what? Once you've committed professional suicide, no one's going to care whose fault it was. Your career will have gone down the tubes—end of story.'

'But... but what's going to happen to me?'

'Well, you *may* be able to make some money doing a kiss-and-tell series for the tabloid press,' Laura had told her with a shrug. 'But that's about it, I'm afraid.'

While Melissa—mercifully silent at last!—had gazed at her in stunned shock and horror, Laura had picked up the phone and ordered some strong black coffee to be sent up straight away.

'OK, I think it's about time we cut out all this nonsense,' she told the other woman. 'So why don't you go and wash your face? Not only will it make you feel a whole lot better, but I'm sure you don't want any of the hotel waiters to see you in this state. And when you come back,' Laura had added with grim determination, 'we're going to sit down and work out how to save your career. Right?'

'Y-yes, all r-right,' the other woman had stuttered tearfully, before stumbling into the bathroom.

However, as she now watched Melissa sipping her hot coffee, and waited to hear whether she was prepared to pull herself together, Laura knew that this was likely to be merely the lull before another storm. But she had to try and get this silly woman to see sense. Because Jack was quite right. Melissa really *was* a great actress—even if her best performances seemed to take place off the set.

'We haven't had a chance to get to know each other very well. But it's important that you realise I'm not just here to read you the Riot Act,' Laura told the other woman quietly. 'In fact, I've actually got quite a lot of sympathy for you. It must have been a terrific shock to discover that Craig was up to his usual tricks.'

'I didn't *know* he was like that,' Melissa muttered, staring dolefully down at the cup in her hands. I . . . well, I was just swept off my feet. He's young and virile— and *so* handsome . . .' she added with a sob, tears beginning to trickle down over her cheeks once again.

'Hang about! You're hardly in your dotage,' Laura retorted briskly, determined to try and keep their discussion on an even keel. 'You may be in your early thirties—'

'Twenty-eight, *if* you don't mind!'

'—but you're still a very lovely, stunningly beautiful woman,' she continued, calmly ignoring the actress's sharp interjection, since practically everyone in the theatrical world automatically lied about their age. 'Jack tells me that he's seen the first few days' rushes and you looked fabulous.'

'Really?'

'Yes, *really*!' Laura grinned. 'In fact, to quote his very words, "she really lights up the screen". Which is why it's *so* important to get you back in front of the camera.'

'Well . . . I *do* want to be in this film,' Melissa assured her, hunting for a handkerchief to blow her nose. 'You know *just* how mad keen I was to play Lady Macbeth. But...but I don't see how I can. Not now. I mean...how could I possibly face Craig? Let alone act with the swine. All the film crew are bound to be so cross and furious with me, as well. I don't think I can bear it!'

Relieved to note that the actress was now regarding her young, unfaithful lover in a more realistic light, Laura pointed out that, despite her feelings about Craig, everyone else on the set would be highly delighted to be getting on with their jobs. 'You'll just have to grit your teeth—and give the performance of a lifetime.'

'What performance?' Melissa grumbled. 'I can't tell you what a mess my hair is in after filming in all that rain. And, even if the rushes are good, darling, I *still* don't think I can face that bloody man Craig Jordan.'

'Of course you can!' Laura snapped, struggling to keep her temper. 'In fact, if you *don't* act him off the screen and completely steal the film from under his nose, you *definitely* aren't the woman I took you for!'

To her surprise, Melissa responded to the tough, exasperated words with an obviously genuine peal of laughter. 'On the principle that revenge is sweet?'

'Well, it can sometimes be a two-edged sword,' Laura admitted, recalling her various encounters with Jack. Which prompted her to add, 'I know that facing Craig isn't going to be easy. But we *all* have to face difficulties in life. I mean, it's thanks to you that I've been forced to spend time up here with your ex-husband. And, believe me, that's a situation I *really* could have done without.'

Even as she found herself saying the words, Laura knew that she should have kept her mouth shut. But it was clearly too late, as Melissa quickly raised her head at the raw, unhappy note in the younger woman's voice.

'Darling! Don't tell me that you've fallen in love with Jack?' Melissa's eyes widened as Laura remained obstinately silent. 'Oh, yes—I can see you *have*. He's lethally attractive, isn't he?' the actress added with a surprisingly warm, sympathetic smile. 'Still, I can't tell you what a relief it is to know that I'm not the *only* one to make a fool of herself.'

'Thanks!' Laura muttered grimly.

'Oh, darling—I'm sorry. I honestly didn't mean to sound so bitchy. And maybe you really *are* the one for him. Come on—tell all!'

'There's nothing to tell,' Laura retorted stonily. 'Especially when your ex-husband hasn't the first idea about caring for someone—or the true meaning of the word "commitment".'

'Well . . . I don't know about that,' the older woman mused. 'He certainly stuck with me for far longer than I deserved. We were absolutely chalk and cheese, of course. And *so* young! But I really think, looking back after all these years, that the main reason I married Jack was simply to get away from home.'

'Oh, come on, Melissa—you aren't seriously trying to tell me . . .?'

'I know that it's an awful thing to say.' She gave Laura a slightly shamefaced, guilty smile. 'I was very fond of my parents, of course. But unfortunately they were dead set against me going on the stage. There were so many rows at home about me having anything to do with such a "wicked profession" that I got really fed up. So when I met Jack, who seemed keen to marry me *and* allow me to get on with my career...' Melissa sighed. 'Well, it just seemed a good idea at the time.'

'But not exactly the best reason for getting married,' Laura murmured drily.

'You're right, it certainly wasn't! We found that out almost straight away. And quite honestly, darling, I'm not exactly cut out for marriage,' the other woman admitted with a shrug. 'I get bored so easily, you see. Jack was working hard—out and about all the time—while I was helping him out in the office, until a good part came along. So having an affair with Donald was just a way to pass the time—if you see what I mean?'

'Mmm...' Laura murmured noncommittally, realising that it was pointless to try and explain to this talented, lovely but basically flawed woman that normal people did *not* have rip-roaring love affairs 'just to pass the time'.

'Luckily, over the years we've managed to forge a rather distant sort of friendship,' Melissa continued, happily unaware of the younger woman's strong disapproval of her way of life. 'Unfortunately, Jack isn't half as resilient as I am. He really *did* get badly hurt in the process. In fact, I'm sure that's why he hasn't ever married again.

'You won't believe this,' she added with a shake of her dark head. 'And he may have calmed down now, of course. But at one time he was almost paranoiac about not allowing any of his staff to become involved with each other, or with their clients.'

'He hasn't changed,' Laura told her grimly.

Melissa sighed. 'I must admit that I've always had a bit of a bad conscience about Jack. I didn't mean to hurt him, but I suppose I can be a first-class bitch sometimes.'

'Only sometimes...?'

'Oh, all right!' The actress gave rueful snort of laughter. 'I guess I deserved that. Especially since I've put you through the hoops today. But I'll bet that you haven't had the experience of actually *seeing* Jack busy making love to a young floozy? And only a few days after he'd professed undying love?' she added bitterly. 'Is it any wonder that I felt *totally* devastated?'

Laura shook her head. 'No, it isn't,' she agreed quietly. 'And you're quite right. I may have had a lot of problems with Jack, but nothing quite as bad as what you've been through. Which is why I've a lot of sympathy for you. And why I want you to get out there and show everyone—not just that rat Craig Jordan—that *you're* the star of this particular show. George Davidson is one of the best directors around today. And, given half a chance, he's going to make a really great film. Quite frankly, I'd like you to be in it!'

'OK, OK, you can stop nagging!' Melissa muttered. 'I just wanted everyone to know that I'd been deeply, *deeply* hurt—that's all,' she added pettishly, before moving over to her dressing table and beginning to brush her long black hair. 'However, despite what you might think, I'm not entirely a fool. So of course I'm going to be on set tomorrow. I'll act that miserable creep Craig "lover boy" Jordan off the stage!' She banged her brush down viciously on the table. 'Just see if I don't!'

Laura grinned. 'I'm relieved to hear it!'

'Yes, well, don't laugh too soon.' Melissa spun around on her stool. 'Because even I know that you're going to have your work cut out getting Jack to the altar.'

'Me? Marry Jack? I've never heard anything so ridiculous!'

'Don't bother trying to kid me.' Melissa gave the younger woman a cat-like grin. 'Between these four walls, you and I both *know* you have every intention of marrying the slippery man! Your problem is how to get the idea into his thick head—right?'

'Absolutely *wrong*!' Laura protested.

'OK, OK...have it your own way.' Melissa grinned at the deep flush spreading over the younger girl's cheeks. 'But if it's any consolation I reckon I'd put my money on you every time. You're certainly tough and resourceful enough to cope with Jack. Just look at the way you've handled me, for heaven's sake!'

'Ah—but then you had every intention of eventually going back on set,' Laura flashed back grimly.

'Yes, I may have. But you didn't know that—not for certain. In fact, the more I think about it, the more I'm convinced that you'd be *perfect* for Jack.' Melissa smiled happily, obviously enjoying the prospect of playing the new role of fairy godmother. 'The poor lamb. He deserves a little happiness at last. I'll have to see what I can do to bring you two together. I can almost hear the heavenly chorus as you plight your troth. It would make a wonderful film, darling; it really would.'

Laura nearly groaned aloud. She needed this daft woman playing Cupid like she needed a hole in the head!

'If you say *one word* to Jack you're dog meat!' she told Melissa bleakly. 'And you can forget any ''heavenly chorus'' nonsense. Just in case you've forgotten—that so-called ''poor lamb'' of yours has Van Gogh's ear for music!'

But Melissa merely threw back her lovely head and roared with laughter, before stating that she would—as promised—be on set first thing in the morning. However, Laura noted grimly, the irritating woman had carefully avoided giving any promises regarding her ex-husband. So it was obviously a case of keeping her fingers crossed and hoping that, once back at work, Melissa would be far too busy to bother with her new agent's private life.

Walking along the sea front of the small fishing port, Laura was glad of Jack's arm. His injunction to 'wrap up warm' had been a timely reminder, on leaving the restaurant, that the wind coming in off the North Sea was still blowing as hard as ever.

'I don't reckon there's anything on the map between us and Siberia,' she muttered, shivering as they were buffeted by another icy blast of wind as they made their way back to his car.

'Let's be positive.' Jack grinned down at her. 'The good news is that it's stopped raining—for a while, at least.'

'Mmm...that is a mercy,' she agreed. 'Although I certainly shouldn't grumble, because I've really taken to Northumberland. No wonder George Davidson was mad keen to use this area for location shots; it may be wild and rugged, but it's spectacularly beautiful. Have we far to go to my hotel?' she added, suddenly feeling very tired after such an early start to what had proved to be a traumatic day.

'Well, it isn't exactly a hotel—more of an old pub, really,' he explained. 'But I think you'll like The Galleon. It has the most amazing collection of nautical objects, and a wonderful view across the harbour, out over the North Sea.'

'I'm sure it will be great. But I honestly don't care if it's a tin shack—just as long as I can get a good night's sleep. Quite frankly I'm practically dead on my feet.'

It hadn't just been a matter of pulling Melissa back into line. As soon as that had been accomplished, she'd not only had to report the good news to the director of the film, but had also spent a considerable amount of time waiting around, principally for Jack to report on the outcome of his negotiations with Craig. Unfortunately, it seemed that the actor had attempted to dig his heels in, and the discussion had been long and protracted, before Jack had grimly announced that his client *would* be appearing on set tomorrow morning.

By the time everything had been sorted out, it had obviously been far too late for her to catch a train back to London. So Jack had promised to find her a bed for the night, as well as insisted on taking her out to dinner. 'You've had one hell of a day,' he'd told her firmly. 'The least I can do is to make sure that you have a decent meal.' And it had definitely been a good idea, because she was now feeling not only full of good food and probably a lot more red wine than was wise, but also thoroughly relaxed and at peace with the world.

'George Davidson is over the moon at being able to get back to work,' Jack said as he unlocked the car. 'He said to tell you that he's thinking of putting your name on the film's credits!'

'I should live so long!' she grinned as he held open the passenger door. 'However, I imagine that sorting out Melissa was a piece of cake compared to dealing with dear Craig.'

'You're right.' Jack sighed and shook his head. 'What a stupid idiot that man is—completely dead wood from the waist up! However, when I made it clear that if he *didn't* eat humble pie and publicly beg Melissa's pardon for his sins his career was finished, he *finally* got the message.'

'How long, do you think, before he's back to his old tricks?'

'Well, let's see . . .' Jack grinned, settling himself into the driver's seat and doing up his seat belt. 'Craig's had a bad fright this time. So I reckon it could be at least two whole weeks before he gets involved with another woman.'

'That long? Wow!' She gave a low whistle of mock surprise, before they both dissolved into peals of cynical laughter.

'Oh, Laura—I must say that it *is* good to spend time with you once again,' he said softly, reaching across to take hold of her hand. 'I've missed you *so* much—and the office hasn't been the same without you.'

'Oh, really?' she murmured, glad of the darkness which hid her flushed cheeks as he gently stroked her fingers. 'Well, luckily, I'm feeling in far too good a mood to remind you exactly *why* and *how* I was sacked from your office. Besides, what about luscious Felicity Green? The girl who's apparently so "easy on the eye", and whom you've been busy seeing lately—both night and day, if what I read in the newspapers is anything to go on.'

'Oh, come on!' he drawled smoothly. 'Surely you don't believe any of that drivel in the Press? Besides, you can't possibly be jealous of Felicity. She's just a nice girl—that's all.'

'Who's talking about being jealous?' Laura snapped, quickly withdrawing her hand from his clasp. 'Not me, buster!'

'Now calm down, Laura. There's no need to—'

'I'm *perfectly* calm,' she ground out through clenched teeth. 'Just as I'm *quite* sure that Felicity is a very nice girl, and making a *great* success of my old job. All right?'

'Oh, yes—absolutely,' he agreed in a maddeningly bland, silky voice which she found deeply irritating. How was it that this man could get under her skin in five seconds flat?

'All the same, Jack, you really did me a great favour,' she murmured in a dulcet tone, quickly deciding that two could play at this particular game. 'If you *hadn't* sacked me, I'd never have started up my own firm. So I guess I owe you a vote of thanks for setting me on the road to what, I hope, will prove to be a very successful business.'

'I've no doubt that you'll achieve it,' he replied coolly as he started the car. 'In fact, you're doing so well that I may have to raid your office and steal your list of clients!'

'I don't think you've got too much to worry about—not *just* at the moment,' she admitted. 'Although, in a year or two, I'm intending to give you a *real* run for your money!'

'There's no need to wait that long, sweetheart,' he murmured, his shoulders shaking with wry amusement. 'Because you can now take Craig off my hands—any time you like.'

All set for her usual war of words with this maddening man, Laura found herself, as she did so often in their turbulent relationship, suddenly having trouble keeping a straight face. 'He really *is* awful, isn't he?' she giggled.

'Absolutely appalling!' Jack agreed, with a low rumble of laughter. 'Luckily, the great British public have no idea that their idol has such feet of clay. And I suppose that Melissa is equally lucky to have discovered the truth before it was too late. I don't imagine that she'll have any trouble with him in the future.'

'No, indeed,' Laura agreed as the car drew up outside a grey stone building. 'Especially as she now fully intends to steal *every* scene in the film!'

They were both laughing as they entered the saloon bar of The Galleon, Laura happy to leave Jack to sort out her room as she gazed about her in amazement.

The large area was simply festooned with fascinating objects, all connected with the sea and ships. Hanging from the ceiling, walls and bar were model boats, fishing gear, ships' wheels, oars, brass lamps, a ship's figurehead and much, much more. In fact, for one mad moment, she seriously wondered if all that wine she'd had to drink during dinner was making her see double. However, Laura soon realised that the bar really *was* awash with nautical antiques.

She was just inspecting a large round diving helmet, when Jack returned to escort her up to her room.

'I wish I'd had the sense to put a toothbrush in my handbag this morning,' she said as they mounted the stairs, pausing on the landing to admire a large collection of model boats, before he led her down the hall and opened a door.

'Oh, this is great!' Laura sighed with pleasure as she viewed a large, comfortable-looking four-poster bed, then went through to inspect the *en suite* bathroom. 'And there's no need for me to borrow your toothbrush,' she added, coming back into the room. 'Because there's already one, plus some toothpaste, in a glass by the basin.'

'Yes, I know. It's mine.'

'Well, that's very thoughtful,' she murmured sleepily. 'And now, if you don't mind, I think it's time I went to bed.'

'Of course I don't mind,' he drawled, his mouth twitching in silent humour as he shrugged off his casual hacking jacket and loosened his tie, before walking across the room to open the door of a large oak wardrobe.

It took some time before the message reached her weary brain. But, as he removed a spare hanger from amongst the suits and shirts hanging in the cupboard, Laura finally began to gain some glimmer of the true situation.

'Now *just* a minute!' she protested, plonking herself down on the end of the bed and glaring at the man who was now casually placing the loose change from his pockets on top of a chest of drawers. 'This is *my* room, and—'

'No. I'm afraid it isn't,' he told her smoothly, his eyes gleaming with unconcealed mockery. 'And, before you say anything else, let me tell you that—other than by bribery and corruption—there's *no way* I could have found you a room for tonight.'

'I...I simply don't believe you!' she groaned, wondering what on earth she was going to do. If there wasn't a spare room, here in this inn, she was going to be in serious trouble.

'Whether you believe me or not, it's a fact,' he retorted firmly. 'When the whole paraphernalia of the film crew and their assorted suppliers—caterers, drivers, sound recordists, et cetera—all descended on this sparsely inhabited area, they took just about *every* available piece of accommodation for miles around. In fact, I only got this room by the skin of my teeth, thanks to the chief cameraman's wife giving birth to a baby—which means that he's gone back to London for a few days. So you can like it or lump it—but that's the situation in a nutshell.'

'I'm *not* sharing this room with you... you conniving bastard!' she ground out furiously.

'OK, Laura—please yourself,' he drawled sardonically, tossing a bunch of keys onto the bed beside her. 'There's nothing to stop you spending the night in the car.'

Scowling at the rotten man, who was now calmly sitting down on a chair and removing his shoes and socks, Laura realised that she was well and truly over a barrel.

It was all right for Jack. Since he'd been driving, he hadn't touched a drop of alcohol, and was now as sober as a judge. But of course she'd had a fair amount of delicious red wine with her meal. Which she now realised had been a grave mistake, because her tired, slightly woozy brain was obstinately refusing to come up with any solution to the problem.

He probably was right about the film people having appropriated all the local accommodation. However, it didn't alter the fact that Jack had deliberately chosen *not* to tell her about the lack of available beds until it was far too late. Was this man a devious, artful and scheming rat—*or what*?

'Well? Have you made up your mind? I think you'll find the car quite comfortable. A little cold, of course,' he drawled mockingly, 'but otherwise perfectly adequate. However, it might be a good idea to take one of these blankets with you. I'll do my best to arrange a hot cup of tea in the morning, and—'

'Oh, *shut up!*' she ground out, almost choking with fury—mostly at herself for having been so easily duped. 'If you think your damned car is so "perfectly adequate", why don't *you* spend the night there?'

'Forget it!' he laughed, taking off his tie and beginning to slowly unbutton his shirt. 'This is *my* bed. And, since I'm a great believer in the equality of the sexes...'

'Do me a favour!' she snarled. 'You've never been anything but a dyed-in-the-wool male chauvinist pig!'

'...I'm quite willing to share my bed with you,' he continued smoothly. 'However, I have *no* intention of sleeping either on the floor or out in my car.'

Laura stared at him grimly for a moment, well aware that the foul man was laughing at her, behind that bland expression on his handsome face. Unfortunately, she could see no way round the problem. Especially when, like Jack, she didn't fancy spending a cold, uncomfortable night huddled on the back seat of his car—however luxurious the leather upholstery might be.

'Oh, all right!' she exclaimed bitterly, accepting her defeat with a heavy sigh. 'I'm cold, tired and fed up. So it doesn't look as if I've got any choice.'

'Sensible girl,' he murmured.

'You can cut out that patronising tone,' she was stung into retorting. 'And I'm going to need a nightgown, so you'd better hand over one of those expensive silk shirts of yours which I can see hanging in the wardrobe.'

'Anything else?' he enquired sardonically.

'Yes. Don't even *think* of trying any funny business. Because if you do I'll scream blue murder and cause one hell of a rumpus! Do I make myself clear?' she demanded.

'Crystal-clear,' he agreed with a grin.

'Good!' she snapped, before whipping the shirt out of his hands and whisking herself into the bathroom, quickly locking the door behind her.

Using her anger as a shield, Laura resolutely refused to let herself even think about having to spend the night in bed with Jack. Quite apart from anything else, she was very tired. In fact, as soon as her head hit the pillow, she was bound to fall immediately into a deep sleep.

On the other hand, if it was really all that simple and straightforward, why was she still sitting on this stool in the bathroom, nervously biting her nails? she asked herself some twenty minutes later.

Come on—stop being so pathetic, she told herself firmly. Jack's obviously every bit as tired and weary as you are. So it really isn't likely that he's going to leap on you with a merry cry. In all probability, the rotten man is already dead to the world—and happily snoring his head off.

CHAPTER NINE

SLOWLY opening the door, and inching silently into the bedroom, Laura almost sagged with relief to discover that she'd been quite right. While Jack wasn't actually snoring, it was obvious from the quiet, regular breathing of the figure lying with his back to her on the far side of the four-poster bed that he was indeed sound asleep.

Grateful for the bright shaft of moonlight streaming in through the open window, which helped her to avoid stumbling into the furniture, Laura tiptoed across the thick carpet, before easing herself carefully into bed.

The mattress was wonderfully soft and comfortable; there was a fragrant aroma of lavender from the lace-trimmed pillow, and as she nestled beneath the warmth of the goose-down quilt she could only be profoundly grateful that she hadn't after all, in a fit of pique, opted for the cold discomfort of Jack's car.

As she was drifting quietly in that timeless space when one is neither awake nor yet asleep, it was some time before Laura became fully aware of the warm fingers gently sliding up and down over the soft silk covering her backbone. It was such a gentle, soothing touch that she was almost purring with contentment and pleasure before she realised that the hand had, somehow, slipped beneath the shirt and was now moving slowly over her bare skin.

'Stop it, Jack!' she mumbled sleepily. 'You promised . . . you promised that there wouldn't be any funny business.'

'So I did. But, my darling one, if you think this is "funny",' he murmured softly in the darkness, 'I don't believe we're talking the same language!'

Whatever the language, it was proving almost impossible to ignore his sensual, erotic caress as his fingers slid over her slim waist and slowly . . . so slowly . . . up towards the curve of her full breasts.

'Besides, how can I possibly go to sleep with your lovely body lying so temptingly beside me?' he breathed, pulling her close to him. 'I want to make love to you, sweetheart,' he added in a low, throbbing whisper which sent her pulses racing out of control. 'So there's no need to yell or scream blue murder. Because I truly love you, Laura, with all my heart.'

'Who's screaming?' she gasped, trembling with excitement as he began brushing his fingers enticingly over her hard, swollen nipples. 'Oh, Jack—do you really mean it? Do you *truly* love me?'

'Really, truly—and very dearly,' he murmured softly as he turned her around to face him, swiftly undoing the buttons of the silk shirt before covering her trembling limbs with his hard, naked body. 'I've been nearly out of my mind at times, wanting you so much,' he added with a muffled groan, burying his face in her soft breasts.

She shuddered uncontrollably at the hoarse sound of his voice, the touch of his lips on her skin sending tremors of delight shivering through every fibre of her being. Free at last of all constraints, she relished the firmness of his body, the hard muscles of his thighs and the strength of the arms clasping her so tightly to him. She had never felt more vibrantly alive, the cool night air from the open window gently fanning their two naked figures as they became caught up in a sudden whirlwind of overwhelming desire.

There was nothing gentle or restrained about their lovemaking. So many months had gone by, with neither of them being able to fully express their powerfully strong, sexual need of one another, that they now seemed gripped by a raw, savagely untamed hunger, sheer lust and passion exploding like atomic fusion as their two bodies merged in a fiercely wild, ecstatic peak of emotional frenzy.

'Oh, sweetheart—I'm sorry,' he muttered as they lay drowsily replete in each other's arms. 'I'm afraid I was far too greedy just now, but it's been *such* a long time since we made love.'

'Well...I'm not exactly complaining!' she murmured, feeling as though she was drifting on a tideless ocean of languid contentment. 'In fact, I'll definitely give you a straight A for effort,' she teased.

'Well, in that case, maybe we ought to try for alpha-plus?' he drawled softly, leaning over to trail his lips down over her throat and breasts.

'For heaven's sake, Jack! Not *again*...' she gasped, amazed to feel the pulsating, hot excitement beginning to ripple through her once more.

'Is that a statement—or a question?'

She was breathless with desire, her heart racing and pounding as his mouth moved slowly down over her quivering body, his tongue exploring every secret curve and crevice, until she was once more moaning helplessly, every nerve-end vibrating with the erotic touch of his lips.

'It's definitely not . . . not a question!' she managed to croak huskily, before swiftly sinking beneath a rushing tide of excitement and the deep, pulsating need to yield to the possession of his powerfully exciting body. Panting for release from the ever-increasing tension which seemed to fill her whole being, she eagerly welcomed the strong, thrusting force of his velvet hardness, their hearts thudding and pounding in unison, until they climaxed together in an explosion of overwhelming passion.

Living in the middle of London, Laura was unused to being woken by a dawn chorus of birds outside her window. She slowly opened her eyes. Noting that the pale grey, early morning light was already stealing into the room, she languorously stretched her body, relishing the comforting weight of Jack's arm lying across her waist.

Blinking hazily up at the pleated silk covering the top of the four-poster bed, she smiled as her mind filled with memories of last night and her own totally abandoned response to Jack's lovemaking. He must have been disturbed by her movement of remembered pleasure, as his arm tightened to pull her towards his hard body, and he sleepily grunted with satisfaction at the close proximity of her warm flesh to his own.

When she opened her eyes again, Laura discovered that she was now alone in the bed, only the rumpled condition of the cool linen sheet providing evidence that Jack had spent the night beside her. For some reason, her head was now feeling extraordinarily thick and heavy, and as she struggled to think where he could be she heard a small, rustling sound on the other side of the room.

'Jack...?' she muttered, quickly sitting up in bed—and then equally quickly wished that she hadn't. 'My *head*!' she groaned softly, feeling as if someone was banging away in her brain with a large, heavy sledgehammer.

Oh, Lord! She must have drunk *far* too much wine last night, Laura told herself, desperately wishing that she hadn't been such a fool. Placing a trembling hand on her aching forehead, she peered across the room at Jack's tall figure, now clothed in a dark silk dressing gown. He was standing with his back to her and it seemed as though he was busy rifling through her handbag.

Struggling to make sense of the scene in front of her, Laura's painful head couldn't seem to cope with the sudden flood of questions. Was that really her handbag? If so, what could he possibly want from it? Jack must have a perfectly good address book of his own. So why...*why* did he have her large business Filofax in his hand?

'What on earth are you *doing*?' she demanded, wincing at the shrill sound of her voice, which seemed to be reverberating loudly in her head. But when he gave a startled, guilty-looking jump of surprise at her words Laura suddenly realised *just* what he'd been up to.

'I...I don't believe it!' she cried, desperately trying to ignore the pounding agony in her head as she jumped out of bed, stumbling across the floor to seize the Filofax from his hands. 'How *could* you do such a thing?'

'Do what?' He frowned down at her. 'I was only looking for my—'

'We both know what you were looking for—you swine!' she cried. 'You didn't mean any of that "I love you'' business last night. It was just a bit of flannel to lull me into a false sense of security. Right?'

'For God's sake, keep your voice down,' he muttered as her raucous tones seemed to echo around the room. 'I don't know what you're talking about.'

'I'm talking about you helping yourself to my business Filofax,' she hissed savagely. 'You warned me last night that you might have a go at stealing my clients. Only I— what a fool!—I thought you were only joking.'

'Of course I was,' he snapped.

'Oh, yeah?' She gave a high-pitched, cynical laugh as she waved the black leather book in front of his face. 'So, what was this doing in your hand? As far as I'm concerned, what we've got here is serious industrial espionage—and I'm not going to let you get away with it!'

He stared at her in astonishment for a moment, before giving a snort of angry laughter. 'Don't be such a damn fool, Laura,' he ground out curtly. 'To claim that I'm the slightest bit interested in any of your clients is nothing but absolute rubbish.'

'*Rubbish?*' she yelled, quickly grabbing her clothes and handbag then dashing towards the bathroom. 'I should have *known* not to trust you, since our whole relationship has been nothing more than one...one large heap of garbage!'

'Stop this nonsense and come back here—at once!' he growled, moving menacingly towards her.

'Go away! I'll never, *ever* trust you again,' she cried, before slamming the door in his face and driving the bolt home with a heavy thud.

* * *

Some considerable time later, and by now heartily sick of being virtually a prisoner in the small bathroom, Laura realised that she'd got herself into a really bad fix.

When she'd first raced in here, full of righteous wrath and indignation, she hadn't actually given any thought to what Jack was likely to do. If she'd had time to think about it, she might have assumed that after waiting for her to come out he'd get fed up and go downstairs to have his breakfast. Which would, of course, have given her an opportunity to slip out of the bathroom, grab her coat and shoes—and somehow make her way back to London.

Unfortunately, however, while the theory behind that scenario was perfectly sensible, in practice it didn't seem to be working out like that at all.

Once she'd found herself in the bathroom, it had obviously made sense to have a long, hot bath—the noise of the water conveniently drowning her copious sobs—and to help herself to some aspirins from a small bottle on one of the shelves. Now, half an hour later, thanks to the hot bath and the aspirins, she was feeling in far better shape, and able to evaluate the position in which she found herself.

Unfortunately, once she'd got rid of the thumping headache and was able to think in a positive, logical manner, it was all Laura could do not to groan out loud. Bitterly vowing never to touch another drop of alcohol as long as she lived wasn't any help, either. Not when she was now having to face the really ghastly, horrible realisation that she might well have made an almighty fool of herself.

Yes, her Filofax really *had* been in Jack's hand. She had no doubt about that. But it was no good trying to fool herself. Even when she'd been actively promoting her new business, Laura had known that it would be many, many years before she was able to attract the same high quality of actors and the enormous financial turnover earned by Jack's firm. So, if he hadn't been after her list of clients, what on earth *had* he been doing?

The answer wasn't long in coming.

'All right, you hellcat . . .!' Jack's voice rasped angrily from the other side of the door. 'My patience has finally run out. If you haven't worked out that I was merely holding your Filofax while looking for my car keys— which I threw across to you on the bed earlier last night— then you must be a total idiot!'

Oh, no! Sitting slumped on the bathroom stool, Laura buried her burning face in her hands. He was right. She really *had* been a complete and utter fool. But . . . but how could she possibly go back out there and face him? It simply wasn't possible. Not after all the really stupid, dreadful things she'd said.

However, if she'd hoped that he would just go away and leave her to quietly wallow in abject misery, she was doomed to disappointment.

'You've got ten seconds to make up your mind,' Jack ground out loudly, his voice heavy with threat and menace. 'Either you come out of that damn bathroom or I'm going to get the owner of this pub up here. All he'll need is a good screwdriver and we'll have that door off its hinges in no time at all!'

'I really, *really* hate that awful man!' she muttered to herself in the mirror, knowing full well, of course, that she didn't hate Jack, and was behaving in a disgracefully childish manner. But how was she to get out of this impasse? How to face him and still manage to salvage her pride?

Even as she asked herself the question, Laura realised with a sinking heart that she was sounding *exactly* like that amazingly stupid airhead Melissa Grant. 'And that, if I may say so,' she told her reflection grimly, 'is definitely a fate worse than death.' Far worse, in fact, than facing the music and forcing herself to apologise to Jack. So, like it or not, she had no choice but to go and eat humble pie.

With a heavy, despondent sigh, she drew back the bolt and slowly opened the bathroom door.

In the brief space of time between leaving one room and entering another, Laura was able to see that the bedroom now looked quite different from when she'd left it, well over an hour ago. The bed had been made, the clothes tidied away, and a round table in the far corner of the room was now covered with a bright, checked cloth and laid for breakfast.

Leaning casually against the window-sill, Jack gazed at her, his hooded grey eyes hard and unreadable, giving her no clue as to his innermost thoughts as the silence lengthened between them.

'I...um...I'm sorry. I've made a total fool of myself,' she managed to mumble at last, unable to meet his eyes as she stared fixedly down at the carpet.

'I'm obviously rather deaf this morning,' he drawled, not bothering to disguise the hard, implacable force underlying his words. 'I didn't catch what you just said. Maybe you'd like to repeat it?'

No, I damn well wouldn't! Laura groaned inwardly, ashamed to suddenly find herself feeling close to tears, and desperately wishing that she could be rescued from her misery. But, since Jack was clearly still very angry, she was just going to have to swallow her pride.

'Um...' She cleared her throat. 'I...er...I'm sorry. I owe you an apology for having been such a fool earlier this morning,' she said quietly, still staring down at the pattern on the carpet. 'To tell the truth, I behaved like a blithering idiot,' she added with a heavy sigh. 'I've got no excuse to offer other than the fact that I had a blinding headache and I obviously wasn't seeing straight—either mentally or visually.'

'Good heavens! This all sounds remarkably unlike your normal aggressive self,' he drawled sardonically. 'Are you quite *sure* that you're feeling all right?'

Stung on the raw, Laura sharply raised her head.

Fully intending to tell him to get lost—because if he didn't think much of her apology that was just too bad!—she found herself staring deep into his eyes, her mind suddenly flooded with scattered, flickering images. Not only of their lovemaking in Tahiti, or here in this room last night, but also the amazing patience which Jack had shown over the past few months.

The many times he'd forgiven all the irritating and maddening pinpricks which she'd deliberately scattered his way; the warmth and comfort of his arms when she'd been so frightened in the lift, and—above all—the overwhelming love she had for this difficult and complex man.

'Well?'

'Maybe I really *am* going down with some dreadful disease,' she murmured with a shaky, tearful smile. 'Because I honestly don't want to fight you any more, Jack.

I'm fed up to the back teeth with all the rows and quarrels we've had over the past few months. Not to mention being sick and tired of the stress and strain of not being entirely honest with one another. Who needs it?'

She waved her hands helplessly in the air. 'I don't suppose you'll believe me, but I'm *truly* not the sort of person who enjoys conflict, or gets a kick from scoring points off other people. I just want... I need...

'Oh, hell!' she wailed, turning to run across the room and throwing herself down on the bed, desperately brushing away the weak tears which had suddenly begun trickling down her face.

'It's all right, sweetheart,' he murmured, moving quickly over the carpet, sitting down beside her and swiftly putting his arms about her trembling figure.

'I've been s-such a s-stupid fool!' she cried. 'I don't know *what* I want, but—'

'Hush, darling. There's no need to cry, because I know exactly what you want.' He smiled tenderly down at the quivering girl in his arms. 'In the short term, you need a decent breakfast, before being driven back to London in a comfortable, fast car—followed by a quiet, leisurely dinner at my house in Chelsea and a good night's sleep. How am I doing so far?'

'B-brilliantly,' she sobbed, ashamed of not being able to stop crying, in spite of the deeply comforting warmth and security of his embrace.

'Ah, well...maybe I can try to do just a *little* better than that,' he murmured, taking a large white handkerchief out of his pocket and gently drying the tears from her eyes. 'Although I'm not at all sure that you will agree. Because I'm sorry to say that I think you're going to have to make an honest man of me at last.'

'I'm...*what*?' Laura raised her tear-stained face, gazing up at him in startled confusion. Had he really said...? No, of course he hadn't! Oh, Lord—maybe she really *was* going down with some awful disease, after all?

Jack gave a heavily dramatic sigh. 'Oh, dear; I can see it's all come as a bit of a shock. Well, you win some, you lose some. But that's life, I guess.'

He shrugged. 'Of course there's no way I can *force* you to marry me. Especially if you simply loathe the whole idea. But I do think that you ought to seriously consider the problems which I'm now having to face. We have, after all, spent a night together in this inn— which, incidentally, is also putting up a large proportion of the film crew. Quite frankly, darling—and if only to protect my good name in show business—I do feel that it's only fair of you to do the decent thing and—*ouch*!'

'You beastly...rotten...horrid man!' she cried, drumming her fists on his broad chest, laughing and weeping at one and the same time.

'Really, Laura!' he protested with a grin. 'What on earth has happened to the deeply penitent, sadly forlorn girl who was so tired of fighting me?'

'She's still here—but only just! Because if you think that you're going to get away with such a lousy, offhand proposal you've got another think coming. "Protect my good name" and "do the decent thing"? What *rubbish*!' She glared up at the man she loved so much, struggling to stop herself from joining in the laughter clearly reflected in his gleaming grey eyes. 'Where, I ask myself, are the red roses and gypsy violins? Not to mention one or two choirs of angels, et cetera, et cetera.'

'Where indeed?' he grinned. 'It's definitely beginning to look as if I've slipped up on some of the finer points of etiquette. But then,' he added more seriously, his voice heavy with regret, 'I do seem to have made a complete hash of our relationship, don't I?'

'Oh, darling—it wasn't just you. I'm truly sorry that I've given you such a hard time over the past few months,' she confessed sorrowfully. 'But we seemed to have got ourselves into a sort of vicious circle. And, however much I tried to break out of it, I just managed to make things worse, somehow,' she added sadly.

'There's no need to blame yourself. It was all my own stupid fault.' He sighed heavily. 'Because right from the day you first walked into my office I *knew* that you were going to cause me problems. I don't mean aggravation,' he added swiftly as she stirred restlessly in his arms. 'I'm talking about my own emotional response to a bright young girl with wonderful auburn hair and sparkling green eyes who'd walked so confidently into my office. When I felt my heart give a sudden lurch, I knew it would be fatal to have you around. Who needs that sort of temptation dangled in front of them every working day?'

'But... but I was engaged to be married at the time,' Laura murmured, secretly thrilled at his picture of her as some sort of *femme fatale*.

'So you were,' he agreed. 'And that's the only reason I took you on. Not only were you bright and intelligent, but you obviously weren't likely to be interested in me. So any instant attraction I'd felt could be allowed to die an early death. But you eventually broke off your engagement, and the situation didn't seem to alter—certainly not as far as I was concerned. The longer we worked together, the harder it got to suppress my feelings.

'In the end, of course, I gave in to temptation,' he added with a sigh. 'And even though we only had two days and nights together I knew that I was in serious trouble.'

'They were the two most wonderful days of my whole life,' she cried, throwing her arms about his neck. 'I was *totally* heartbroken when you rejected me. I really couldn't believe it was happening to me! I ... I think I must have been out of my mind with pain and agony.'

'Oh, my love!' he groaned, clasping her tightly to him. 'I was such a fool. God *knows* what possessed me to give you the sack after our trip to Tahiti. All I can say with any certainty is that after flying back to England I spent days and nights wrestling with the problem. Because I'd discovered that I was deeply in love with you, and—'

'Really?'

'Really, truly, deeply and—unfortunately as it turned out—quite madly. And, it's that madness which has, I'm afraid, led to most of our problems over the past months.

'As I saw it, there were really only three or four courses of action open to me. Either I got rid of you straight away, putting all temptation well out of my reach, and concentrated on work until I'd somehow got you out of my system, or we became an item, carrying on our love affair, and probably causing disruption all over the place. Because I could see very clearly, even if you couldn't at the time, that having a member of staff sleeping with the boss was bound to lead to trouble and gossip, both within the industry and, more seriously, in the office.

'So I chose the third alternative: that of removing you from the work environment—and hoping to provide an alternative job so that we could continue to be together.'

'But that was never going to work,' she protested. 'Not unless you'd *told* me how you felt about me...about us.'

'I know.' He shook head at his own folly. 'I did say that I was *madly* in love, didn't I? Because I really think that I must have been temporarily out of my mind at the time. And for some months afterwards,' he added, with a grim bark of unhappy laughter.

'Because, of course, there was always the fourth alternative—that of asking you to marry me. And yes, I certainly thought about it. But...well, my marriage to Melissa had been such a total disaster that I dreaded the thought of making another mistake. In the past, for instance, I'd always made sure that I never got myself into a position where the question might arise.'

Laura laughed. 'That sounds like a case of "Mr Loverman strikes again"!'

'Oh, come on—that's not fair!' he laughed in return. 'Some journalist once coined that phrase in an idle moment—and it's a ghastly tag that's been hung around my neck ever since. However, I've always tried to play fair. It's many years since my marriage broke up, so I'm not going to try and pretend that I've lived like a monk,' he told her with a shrug. 'However, any girlfriends I may have had always knew right from the beginning of the relationship that I was strictly not interested in any serious emotional entanglement. Until you came along and upset all my careful calculations,' he added with a heavy sigh.

'Oh, yes—and what about the lovely Felicity Green?' she demanded, still not entirely convinced that he hadn't fallen, if only temporarily, for the girl with such a truly amazing figure.

'Ah, yes,' he grinned. 'I was *very* encouraged to see just how cross and jealous you were about dear Felicity! Although why you should think that I'd fancy a pneumatic blonde when I was in love with a slim redhead I've absolutely no idea.'

'I wasn't really jealous,' Laura muttered, her cheeks flushing as he gave a low chuckle of laughter. 'Or if I was...just a bit...it's not really surprising. She really is stunning, isn't she?'

'She certainly is!' he agreed with maddening cheerfulness. 'In fact, I went to a lot of trouble to pick *just* the type of girl likely to cause you a few disturbed nights. However, I have to say that I didn't find her at all physically attractive and she bored me rigid. Sad, isn't it?'

'Absolutely tragic,' Laura agreed with a happy grin. 'But why go to all that trouble? I mean, I was already crazily in love with you. So why dangle Felicity in front of my nose?'

'I knew that we were both sexually attracted to one another—but then Donald Hunt suddenly appeared on the scene. You certainly seemed to be *very* close to him. And since he'd already been partly instrumental in breaking up my marriage I was damned if he was going to carry off the girl I loved. Unfortunately, despite trying to be cool and sophisticated about the situation, I saw no reason why *you* shouldn't suffer the same agonies of jealousy that I was going through. Which is why,' he added with a shamefaced smile, 'I dangled Felicity in front of you at every conceivable opportunity.'

Laura threw back her head and roared with laughter. 'It's nice to know that I'm not the only idiot around here. Honestly, Jack—how can you be so blind? It's *Susie* who interests Donald—not me!'

'Oh, dear! Hmm...well, it seems that I may have made a slight miscalculation there.' He laughed. 'Anyhow, once Donald appeared on the scene, I finally decided that I was going to marry you if it was the last thing I did. Only unfortunately it nearly was. Because the reason I was hunting in your handbag for my car keys—which seem to have totally disappeared, by the way—was because I had left what I hoped would prove to be your engagement ring in the glove compartment in my car. You see, I *had* planned to give you the ring this morning. Alas for the best laid plans...'

'And I spoilt it all,' she groaned. 'I'm *so* sorry, darling. How could I have been such an idiot?'

'Well, looking back over our tempestuous love affair, I must say that I'm forced to the conclusion that we've *both* been idiots. So why don't we forget the past and simply look forward to the future?'

'I'll second that,' she agreed fervently. 'The only thing is...what about business? I know you don't think we ought to work together,' she added quickly. 'And it may surprise you to know that I agree with you.'

'Now I *know* you're not well!' he laughed.

Laura grinned. 'OK—less of the wisecracks, if you don't mind! But seriously, Jack—what *are* we going to do?'

'Well, I've obviously given the matter some thought, and I feel that the best solution is to sell my present house and buy something much larger, with a basement or attic, which can be solely devoted to your business.

Because you're quite right—the idea of sharing the same office building is absolutely *out*! And I think pinching each other's clients would have to be grounds for divorce, don't you?'

'You've got no arguments so far,' she said.

'Hmm...you may not be too happy with my final stipulation. I really am going to insist on *strict* working hours—for us both. If you can successfully maintain a balance between your business and our family life, that's fine by me. But, even at the risk of sounding a complete male chauvinist, I want your husband and children to be the most important things in your life—with business well in second place. Am I asking too much?'

Laura gazed at him for a moment, realising that he was quite right. She loved her business. She'd be very unhappy not to be able to continue a career which she loved. But, at the end of the day, there was really no choice. Because, if she'd learned nothing else over the past few months, she was very certain of one fundamental fact: that without Jack by her side life for her had no meaning at all.

'Well?' he demanded, the slight trembling in his hands the only evidence that he wasn't one hundred per cent certain of her answer.

'Oh, I don't know...' Laura muttered, struggling to keep a straight face as his arms tightened possessively about her. 'Maybe we could give it a whirl. The script needs polishing, of course, and you still haven't signed up the leading lady,' she teased. 'But on the whole I'd say the scenario has a certain amount of promise. On the other hand, maybe...'

'There isn't going to be any damn "maybe" about it!' he growled huskily, crushing her fiercely to him, his mouth descending to cover her quivering lips in a kiss of demanding, hungry possession.

'OK, OK... I think I've got the message!' she gasped breathlessly as she lay dazed in his arms some moments later.

'And about time too!' He smiled down at her. 'So are you going to marry me—with or without the gypsy violins?'

'Oh, yes, Jack!' she murmured happily, winding her arms about his neck.

'And you're going to promise to love, honour and obey me—as long as we both shall live...?'

'You've always had my love and honour.' She smiled up into his eyes. 'I'm not so confident about the ''obey'' bit of the marriage vows, of course—but I'll certainly do my best.'

'Hmm... possibly we shouldn't put too much emphasis on the likelihood of obedience?'

'How wise and clever you are, Mr Loverman!' she laughed. 'Although I do promise to *try* and mend my ways.'

He laughed. 'Not too soon or too suddenly, my darling Laura. I really don't think I could stand the shock! Let's just take one day at a time.'

'One day—every day—for the rest of our lives,' she murmured lovingly as he took her lips in a kiss of fierce possession and total commitment.

Take 4 bestselling love stories FREE
Plus get a FREE surprise gift!

FREE VALENTINE'S BROOCH!
$9.95 U.S. retail value

This Valentine's Day Harlequin brings you all the essentials—romance, chocolate and jewelry—in:

VALENTINE *Delights*

Matchmaking chocolate-shop owner Papa Valentine dispenses sinful desserts, mouth-watering chocolates...and advice to the lovelorn, in this collection of three delightfully romantic stories by Meryl Sawyer, Kate Hoffmann and Gina Wilkins.

As our special Valentine's Day gift to you, each copy of *Valentine Delights* will have a beautiful, filigreed, heart-shaped brooch attached to the cover.

Make this your most delicious Valentine's Day ever with *Valentine Delights!*

Available in February wherever Harlequin books are sold.

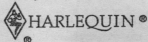

HARLEQUIN ®

Look us up on-line at: http://www.romance.net

VAL9

Jake wasn't sure why he'd agreed to take the place
of his twin brother, nor why he'd agreed to commit
Nathan's crime. Maybe it was misplaced loyalty.

DANGEROUS
Temptation

by *New York Times* bestselling author

Anne MATHER

After surviving a plane crash, Jake wakes up in a hospital
room and can't remember anything—or anyone...
including one very beautiful woman who comes to see
him. His wife. Caitlin. Who watches him so guardedly.

Her husband seems like a stranger to Caitlin—he's full of
warmth and passion. Just like the man she thought she'd
married. Until his memory returns. And with it, a danger
that threatens them all.

Available in February 1997 at your favorite retail outlet.

MIRA The brightest star in women's fiction

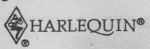